There Was Once a Place

There Was Once a Place
The Fiction Desk Anthology Series
Volume Seven

Edited by Rob Redman

The Fiction Desk

First published in 2014 by The Fiction Desk Ltd.

This collection © The Fiction Desk Ltd.
Individual stories © their respective authors.

This book is sold subject to the condition that it shall not, by the way of trade or otherwise, be lent, resold, hired out, or otherwise circulated without the publisher's prior consent in any form of binding or cover other than that in which it is published and without a similar condition, including this condition, being imposed on the subsequent purchaser.

ISBN 978-0-9927547-2-3

The Fiction Desk
PO Box 116
Rye
TN31 9DY

Please note that we do not accept postal submissions.
See our website for submissions information.

www.thefictiondesk.com

The Fiction Desk Ltd
Registered in the UK, no 07410083
Registered office: 3rd Floor, 207 Regent Street, London, W1B 3HH

Printed and bound in the UK by Imprint Digital.

Contents

Introduction   7
Rob Redman

I Say Papaya, You Say Pawpaw   9
Mike Scott Thomson

Dan and the Dead Boy   21
Mark Taylor

Little Bird Story   33
James Collett

Constructing an Exit   37
Peter Clarke

Misson to Mars: An A–Z Guide   53
Sarah Evans

Contents

Santa Maria *Edmund Krikorian*	59
Colouring In *Cindy George*	75
Badass *Die Booth*	79
The Guy in the Bear Suit *Dan Purdue*	83
The Stamp Works *Alex Clark*	87
Exile *Melissa Goode*	109
The Loop *Chris Fryer*	119
Loss Angina *Nik Perring*	137
Bing Bong *Jo Gatford*	141
About the Contributors	145

Introduction
Rob Redman

Although we don't deliberately theme our anthologies (with the exception of *New Ghost Stories*), themes do present themselves as each collection comes together. There's a synchronicity at work: we might receive no stories set in Rome for a month, and then one day five stories will arrive in a row, from different authors in different countries, and all set in the same piazza.

The emerging themes in this volume draw lines through and around the stories, forming a kind of map of ideas: Chris Fryer and Melissa Goode take very different looks at what it means to revisit lost times and places. Peter Clarke, Nik Perring, and James Collett write about the nature of dependency, whether on substances or on people; Nik Perring also shares a border with

Mike Scott Thomson and Sarah Evans, for the adjustments their characters are making to loss or changed circumstances. Several stories concern themselves with the challenges we face in defining who we are (Die Booth), and in maintaining that definition (Jo Gatford). Other stories might stand out on their own, thematic islands that nevertheless give shape and character to the coastline: sometimes a guy in a bear suit is just a guy in a bear suit (and sometimes it isn't).

We all see our own lines and patterns; your map will be different from mine. But this is fiction, and getting lost is not a problem.

This is Mike Scott Thomson's second Fiction Desk story: 'Me, Robot' appeared in Crying Just Like Anybody. *I can't decide whether this story ends with a flash of optimism or a descent into Orwellian darkness. I suppose it depends on your point of view.*

I Say Papaya, You Say Pawpaw
Mike Scott Thomson

The day I shut up shop for the final time, I cried like a baby. After three generations, Greenacres was no more. To know why, you need only venture to the green belt on the edge of town. There it stands, that recently erected red-brick monstrosity: Megasave.

Shortly afterwards, almost to my surprise, I found I still needed to eat. My mortgage also wasn't going to pay itself. Thus it was that the twin necessities of an empty stomach and an even emptier bank balance sealed my fate. What else was an honest grocer to do?

I was interviewed by Penny, the Powdered Person from Personnel. My name didn't ring a bell. Instead she murmured, eyes down, 'Much retail experience, then?'

It was all I could do not to scoff. Instead I squirmed in my unironed suit and nodded.

Now, every time I pass through those automatic double doors, their electronic groan is how I imagine my dear old father and grandfather would sound as they collectively spin in their graves.

So, this is what I do now. Sit on a hard plastic swivel chair behind the scanner, take things from the belt with my right hand, beep, pass them to my left. Then when I'm done, I press subtotal, swipe their Megasaver's Reward Card, ask for money, put cash in the till or watch them punch in their PIN. Give change, or cashback. Not forgetting the receipt. Customer wanders off with their shopping without so much as a second look in my direction. Likewise, moments later, I don't remember what they look like. Afterwards, it starts again, a new faceless drone passing through my aisle. Scan, beep. Scan, beep. Scan, beep. Eight hours a day.

In front of me, a column of seventeen other people do exactly the same thing. To my rear, ten. This place is a cavern of consumerism, a pantheon of perishables, swallowing the community spirit whole, spitting it out again so it lands with a splat on the sickly yellow tiles, a putrid mess of pips, pulses, and loyalty points. The whole store stinks of rancid bananas and caustic cleaning fluid. Greenacres was earthy, fertile, and vibrant. This makes me want to spew.

At least it reveals what a rich tapestry we have in this country. So far, there's been the two old crones who squawked incessantly to themselves when I forgot to give them a single penny for re-using their tattered old carrier bag. They waited for fifteen whole minutes, tut-tutting all the time, whilst I served the customer next in line before I could open my till again. And did they put that penny in the charity box? Did they? Did they arse.

Then there was that portly, pompous duffer with pebble lenses who got all indignant when I let a large sack of frozen minced beef pass by without first wrapping it inside a clear plastic bag. His considered response was to sling it back in my direction, only for it to split open, spraying its contents all over the conveyer belt and my lap, making till number eighteen resemble the new headquarters of a colony of maggots and me, by extension, King Maggot.

Then, I had that grey old couple who called me a 'disservice to the profession', or something like that, when I broke the devastating news that I'd run out of five pound notes and could they, perhaps, take these coins instead? No, they bloody well couldn't, thank you very much.

And, if the customers themselves weren't enough, to top it all there's the customer services manager, Pamela. Need some assistance with an unknown item, or a declined credit card? Don't count on her help any time soon. If you're lucky, she may come mooching up to your till, lips nonchalantly pursed, as if there's all the time in the world, ten minutes after you ping on your light. Otherwise you have to sit there, sweat prickling the back of your neck under that regulation cream shirt, the customer's frown a laser beam boring through your forehead.

In fact, it's fair to say my new job would be a lot more enjoyable without customers and staff alike. I've been here for little more than a month and, my God, I can't take any more.

Honestly, these days it's whinge, whinge, whinge. That's all I hear. Hardly anyone says a nice word. I say good morning, or good afternoon, or good evening, and my latest customer murmurs a forced response, sniffs, or rustles the carrier bags, eyes down, busy busy busy. One person has been kind. One! A lady. Strawberry blonde hair, faux-fur coat, green beret. Probably my age, forty-ish, maybe a year or two younger, I dunno. She smiled at me, that first day — she was the first customer I served — and she made some passing comment about the weather, as you do. So I told her, hey, you're my first ever customer!

'Really?' she said. 'Well, I'm honoured.' Then she looked at me again and said, 'Don't I recognise you?'

'Used to have that greengrocers in town,' I replied. She frowned, trying to remember, so I said, 'I'm Greenacre. Rob Greenacre.'

'Oh my goodness, right...' Her face coloured as the penny dropped. Like everyone else, she would have stopped going as soon as this sparkling new place came along. She's not the only one I've recognised since coming here. 'Sorry it didn't work out for you...' she offered.

I gave a rueful grin, shrugged.

'Oi!' We turned to an orange-faced woman next in line. 'I don't expect to be made to wait all day whilst you two mooch around gossiping,' she warbled.

'Yes, sorry,' said the lady in the green beret. 'I'll see you around, Rob,' and off she went. I never even got her name.

I looked at the old biddy who'd taken her place and imagined ramming her sticks of rhubarb down her throat.

There's a lull in proceedings, and what do you know? Here comes Pamela. Not as my supervisor, but as a customer.

She places a number of individual, unlabelled items down upon my belt. Mangos, guavas, star fruits, passion fruits, sharon fruits, dragon fruits, kumquats. Four types of apples: Granny Smith, Cox, Pink Lady, Russet. One Conference pear, one Alexander Lucas. A tricolour of grapefruit. A single papaya.

'That's quite some salad you're making,' I exclaim as I type in the code for each one. I don't even have to look them up: that's a lifetime of experience for you. In response, she stares at me, eyes large and vacant like a heifer. She puffs her cheeks and says nothing.

I reach the papaya and punch in its code. Its name flashes on the LED screen.

'Pawpaw,' she pipes up.

I look at the fruit. It's not a pawpaw. It's a papaya. I tell her this.

'That's not how we have it,' she says. 'It's a pawpaw.'

'It's not a pawpaw,' I maintain. 'Pawpaws are big and round. This is small and pear-shaped. See?' I hold it up. 'It's a papaya.'

'Suit yourself,' she says. Like it makes any bloody difference. I punch it in as a papaya.

I scan the next two items, a tube of toothpaste and a copy of *Country Living* magazine, and press subtotal. Immediately Pamela leans forward with a key, sticks it in my machine and cancels the sale.

'Right,' she says, avoiding eye contact. She opens the cardboard tube of toothpaste. 'Two sticks of chewing gum,' she says, sliding them out, 'hidden.' She picks up *Country Living*, tilts it downwards. 'A birthday card – concealed.'

I sit there, speechless. It's like she's punched me in the neck.

'And it is a pawpaw,' she says. 'Close your till. You're on the trolleys.'

Without a word, I get up, log off, and turn out my light. I make a point of taking a long, slow look at her, making sure she sees me and how disappointed I am, as I head through the double doors to the car park.

At least gathering stray trolleys and heaving them across the tarmac is a chance to get some exercise and let off steam. Every time I clank one trolley into another, I turn the air blue.

'Rip the piss out of me, will you?' I mutter under my breath. 'Single me out? Just 'cos I stick out like a sore thumb.' I steer my line of eight trolleys, clang them into a ninth. 'I'll show you a pawpaw, you moon-faced old troll.'

As I steer the chain of trolleys back towards the building, it's then I see them.

First up, it's — well, would you effin' believe it — it's a papaya. Lying on the ground. Must have fallen out of somebody's shopping bag. Of all things! And no, it's not a bloody pawpaw. I bend down to pick it up.

The other thing I've seen is Pamela's car. It's one of those new models of VW Beetle, a hideous electric blue. It's parked near the steps down to the store, facing away from its double doors.

I take a quick look this way and that, then, using my line of trolleys as a shield, wedge the papaya up her exhaust pipe. I don't even have to squeeze it. Fits perfectly. I chortle as I push the trolleys back to the shop.

As I get there, one of the other till monkeys, a young Saturday jobbing lad, is there to meet me. 'I'm taking over,' he says. 'Pamela wants you stacking the juices.'

'Right you are,' I say, heading back inside. She doesn't even have the guts to give me her orders herself. Typical.

But I feel better now, although I can do without the store's rancid smell striking my nostrils again. It's less bad in the chilled section though, and sure enough there's a large pallet of orange juice cartons ready to be placed on the refrigerated shelves. I get to work.

As usual when I'm on the shop floor, I get interrupted. Asked where things are, mainly. I mean, honestly: organic quinoa. Wasabi peas. Vege-bloody-mite. But, I try my best. Nine times out of ten I point them in the right direction.

This time, it's a grinning old lady who has shuffled over asking about orange juice.

'It's right here!' I say, holding one of the cartons aloft. I guess she can't see that well; besides, she's smiling. Makes a change to see a friendly face.

The old lady laughs, a dry rattle, and firmly clasps my arm. 'Ah, but you see,' she says, 'I want the one without the orangey bits.'

'Orangey bits?'

'Yes, orangey bits. They get stuck in my dentures, you see.'

'Ah. Now we can't have that.' I look at my pallet, and the shelves in front of me. They do indeed have fruity bits. I take a look to one side. The smooth varieties are on the next shelf. I take one, handing it over. 'Without the bits!' I exclaim.

She looks at me, then the carton, and her old face breaks into a wonderful smile. Never mind how easy this conundrum was to solve; I flush with unexpected pride, knowing my good deed is done for the day. 'Oh!' she chuckles. She pats my arm with genuine gratitude and takes the carton. I smile back and turn again to the shelves.

Next thing I know, she's breakdancing on the floor.

It happens fast. One moment, she's shuffling to her trolley. The next — crash! — she's tumbled over my pallet, the busted carton of juice gushing in a pool of orange around her, the old bird's two brown-stockinged legs a V-shape in the air.

I gawp. You would think, wouldn't you, that if you see an old lady theatrically succumb to the forces of gravity, you would rush to her aid? But, the shock has paralysed me. And I don't know what to do. I want to help her, sure, but... oh, this is bad. 'Are you okay?' I stammer.

From up the aisle, someone comes huffing and puffing. It's Pamela. She squats down and starts fussing.

'Hello! Mrs Redmond, dear! Taken a tumble, have we? Now then! Do you hurt anywhere? Or are you just shaken up? No? Shall I call an ambulance? No? Shall we sit you on a nice comfy seat somewhere? Fetch you a nice cup of tea? Excellent! Good idea!'

Pamela looks at me. 'Get her a tea.'

She turns back to Mrs Redmond, her shrill speech once more transforming into a flurry of question and exclamation marks. 'Now then! Let's try and get you up! Good girl... one, two, three, hy-hup! Oh, well done! What a surprise that was, huh? How bad things can happen to good people...!'

I saunter off to the staffroom to make a tea. All the while I'm thinking: I'm finished, now. Probably my fault for not moving the pallet out of the way. And I didn't help her. Pamela saw me not helping her. What if she's broken a hip? There'll be damages. I'll be blamed. Yup. I'm finished.

When I come back down, Mrs Redmond is perched on a plastic chair by the fish counter, fanning herself with a *Daily Mail*. She's shaking a little, but otherwise seems to be fine. I hand the tea over.

'Thank you, my sweet,' she says. She glances up at Pamela. 'This gent was ever so helpful, you know.'

'I'm sure he was,' says Pamela, deadpan. She looks at me. 'See you in ten minutes in the interview room.'

I'm forty years old and feel like a naughty schoolboy.

It's as I'm waiting to go in the interview room, hovering tentatively in the corridor leading from the austere staff canteen, that it strikes me how much I need this. Apart from anything else, I'm making money. Granted, not a lot, but enough to scrape by. It's better than nothing. Better than those twice-monthly visits to the Job Centre.

But, it's not simply about money. I get *time* here. This place demands a mere eight hours from me, five days a week. Greenacre's was a full-on twenty-four-seven affair. I never got to do anything else. The only people I ever met were my customers. And even they deserted me in the end.

From along the corridor I hear a familiar huffing and puffing. 'What are you standing outside for?' says Pamela as she reaches me. 'Go in.'

I obey.

I'm surprised to see Penny, the Powdered Person from Personnel, already sitting at the desk. She glances up as I enter and raises her pencilled eyebrows. I think that's a greeting, but I'm not sure. Actually, it appears to be a smile. I do a sort of grimace back. Surely they're not going to take pleasure in this?

I think it best to be the first to speak. 'How's the old lady?'

'Who?' asks Penny.

'She'll live,' pipes up Pamela. 'Old folk round here go topplin' like ninepins. That's the fourth time this month.'

'Oh. Right,' I stammer, unsure. 'So...'

'We wanted to offer you our congratulations,' says Penny.

'What?'

'You came top.'

I look at Penny, her expression unreadable under all those layers of foundation, and Pamela. I'm doubly surprised to see Pamela's expression has cracked into a broad grin. This is too weird. Witnessing a smile on Pamela's languid face is like seeing a handlebar moustache on a baby. Not meant to be. But, there it is.

'Top?' I say. 'Of what?'

'The produce test. Nobody else knew as many as you did. And you whizzed them through in record time, too.' Penny turns to Pamela, who nods. 'You didn't get the hidden items, but nobody did.' She shrugs. 'Orders from head office, you understand.'

'Oh. Right.' I'm guessing I'm not fired after all. 'Well... that's good to know.'

'Anyhow,' says Penny. 'In two weeks' time there'll be a vacancy coming up. Produce Department Manager. I think given your previous experience, it would be prudent to apply. Would you not think so, Mr... Greenacre?'

I exit the room ten minutes later with my head buzzing. Plans and schemes are snapping like miniature lightning bolts through my synapses. Of course, all that sitting on the till was to get a foot in the door. I would defeat this monolithic corporate beast from the inside! And this new post? I'll be a shoo-in.

But, that'll be the beginning. I'll start with getting my name out there, maybe even a subtle rebranding of the fruit and veg section. 'Greenacres at Megasave: local knowledge at your convenience at bargain prices.' Or something like that. Oh, the possibilities! That's all I needed, a bit of impetus. I'll make something of myself here. I'll make my dad and granddad proud. I'll do it for them.

I exit from the staff area back to the store. I don't even detect the rancid stench of rotten bananas any more. This place is a hive of humanity: young and old, large and small, rich and poor, fancy and frugal. It occurs to me that out of all those customers who shunted through my till, I've been the biggest whinger of the lot.

I hear a voice. 'Goodbye!'

Turning to the source of this exclamation, I see an impossibly perky Pamela.

'See you tomorrow!' I respond, giving a little salute.

'But before I go...' she says. Leaning forward, she takes my name badge and peels off the long white sticker, the strip that says 'Trainee'. 'I think it's about time, don't you?' she exclaims, rolling the peeled-off label into a sticky ball. Her tired eyes twinkle from the overhead fluorescent lights; this job has beaten her, but she's hanging on in her own singular way.

I don't do anything other than grin. Pamela nods another goodbye and strolls – leisurely, like she always does – out of the store.

Chuckling to myself, I find I've wandered into the fruit and veg section. Soon to be my new realm; my domain. Yup, I can imagine a cheeky tweak of the Megasave logos here and there. Somehow I'll get my name on it. A bit of fresh enterprise, that's what this place needs. And I have one person to thank. One deceptively lovely lady who has turned my career around. I almost feel guilty about sticking that papaya up her...

Oh, shit.

Right on cue I hear loud, muffled 'pop', followed by a short, clipped cry emanating from beyond the double doors. This time, if there's any shock to paralyse me, it's instantly nullified by a mortifying stab of guilt. I run, legs-a-blur, to the trolley park.

Someone is squatting on the concrete, a hand rubbing the back of her neck. I see a cascade of strawberry blonde hair matted with a splodge of goo, and my heart plummets. A green beret, having been sent flying, is resting by a stack of wire baskets. I bend to retrieve it and look at the stricken lady. She returns my look, her bewildered face a mask of confusion and hurt, and I feel six inches tall. Reaching into my jacket, I pull out some tissues. 'Are you all right?' I say as I hand them over. 'Are you hurt?'

'I don't know what happened,' she says. 'One moment your colleague is giving me a cheery wave as she drives off. Next thing I know, something goes splat on my head.'

From my position kneeling on the ground, I catch sight of Pamela's electric blue VW Beetle exiting to the main road, its driver oblivious to the scene left in its wake. Nearby, shuffling up the pathway to the double doors, are two old women. What's strange is that I recognise them. They're the same ones who waited fifteen minutes for that one measly penny. They don't pay us any attention, but I can hear them grumbling about something.

I sigh. Bad things really do happen to good people. If you let them.

The lady examines her sticky hand. 'What on earth is it?'

I'm about to lie and say 'no idea' when I change my mind. 'Looks like it was a pawpaw,' I say.

'Are you sure?' she asks as she sniffs at the mess. 'I would say a papaya.'

'I suspect,' I say, 'that if you break them apart, you'll find they're pretty much the same.'

Mark Taylor's first story for The Fiction Desk takes a perceptive look at the way we relate to the people around us – and the people inside us.

Dan and the Dead Boy
Mark Taylor

Lying in recovery after my first satisfying piss in three years, I ran my fingers over the dressing on my belly and imagined sliding them through the incision to tear out the dead boy's kidney. I saw it flop off the bed, a bloody half-moon left behind on the sheet, and landing on the floor to be carried off by a cleaner; and my body being mine again. They say it might last ten years. A decade with it, as my blood runs through and becomes his blood.

Mum said that the transplant would change me. She said I would take on the dead boy's personality, start reading superhero comics and take up the guitar. She said that nobody knows how it works, but a woman in America who had crippling vertigo started taking her new kidney up mountains and later discovered the donor was a daredevil. Perhaps she was right, and this is how the boy who saved my life used to feel. Aren't all teenagers this self-centred and ungrateful?

I thought it was the world that would change. Before the operation, I thought the colours would be bolder and strangers would smile wider. Lying there with the new kidney weighing me down, I knew that the colours would be duller and strangers would avoid my eyes, knowing what I had taken from the dead boy. Of course, the world was just the same. The hospital was ugly and the car smelled too much of air freshener and my flat was as half-tidy as I left it. In the street, strangers ignored me the way they always had. By the second week back at work, I might never have been ill.

The terrible thing that happened to me is over. I was caught up in a storm, clinging on to a breaking boat and hoping rescue would come before my grip failed. Now that I have been fished out and fixed up and tidied over, I am on my own.

At 10am and 10pm, every day, whatever else I do, I take my immunosuppressants. I have paused with the tablet on my tongue and thought: if I spit it out, if I tip the rest down the toilet, the boy's kidney will die. But I am responsible to a fault. I read the leaflets they gave me five times each, so I know that rejected kidneys don't have to be removed. If I must carry his offal about with me I might as well make use of it. If I let his kidney die, then I will go back on dialysis. It's comforting to think of, but even on my worst days I remember how miserable dialysis was, even when the tube in my abdomen had become a part of me.

Much of the rest of my time is spent avoiding damp hay. This is very important. I know it is very important because I read those leaflets so carefully, and in the dead hours when the fluid was draining from my belly I made intricate plans for how I would keep myself away from damp hay. If it is unavoidable that I handle damp hay, I must wear disposable gloves and a mask, but I don't intend to let things go that far.

I must avoid damp hay because my immunosuppressants mean it might kill me. I might succumb to the hay infection and turn into a scarecrow.

The difficulty is that damp hay rarely figured in my life before the transplant, so I don't know where to expect it. It could be lurking around any corner. There could be a bale of it under my bed. And any dry hay I come across could become damp at any time, with just a shower of rain or a spilled drink. What kind of life is it, always on the lookout for hay and for moisture? How could I ever raise a family like this?

Despite these demands on my time, I have taken on a few new hobbies, though I doubt any of them are the dead boy's. The first is drinking. Not alcohol, not even coffee: just water, by the pint, by the gallon. On dialysis, drinking water can kill you. You fill up from the ankles until it reaches your lungs and you drown from the inside. Now I can occupy myself with pouring water down my throat. But I keep thinking: I am making the dead boy earn his lodgings. I don't want to think that. It distracts me from distraction.

Another is writing letters to the dead boy's family. They don't let you send many, and it's like writing home from the trenches: the censors in the transplant team look over every word to make sure you aren't compromising confidentiality. I've written one, officially, and it was the hardest thing I've ever done, lying like that.

> Dear family,
>
> My name is Dan and I'm twenty-seven years old. A letter can't begin to convey how grateful I am for the gift I have been given. I was on dialysis for sixteen months and I had started to think that would be the whole rest of my life.

Your son has given me the chance to live a real life. I will use it in a way that you and he would be proud of.

I know that nothing I can write to you would ease the pain of your loss, but I hope you can find consolation in the knowledge that through that loss, a life has been saved.

You are in my thoughts, and will be every day.

Thank you,

Dan

I copied most of that from the Internet. I don't think the censors are too worried about plagiarism. It was the only way I could get to the end. But the others, the ones I don't send, those are easy.

Dear family,

Your boy is dead and buried now, but parts of him are not buried in the ground, they are buried in people like me. They are living on beyond their time, long past when they should have rotted. Doesn't it make you sick, to know that your son is walking around in a dozen different bodies, like some strange undead thing?

It makes me sick to know that I am keeping this part of him alive.

My name is Dan and I am twenty-seven years old. That means that I will need another kidney, maybe two or three, before I die. In a decade's time I will have this thing out of me and a new one put in its place, like changing a lightbulb, and perhaps the new one will fit.

Until then, please accept my sincere condolences for your loss.

Yours faithfully,

Dan

They always say that you can go on holiday while you're on dialysis. They go on and on about how you can live a normal life, or near normal, just as long as you make sure that there's a local hospital that knows you're coming, and you spend hours of every day dialysing, and you don't eat or drink anything you might actually enjoy. Pleasure is bad for renal health. That's why cranberry juice is so good for you.

I never bothered. But once it had got used to me, the dead boy's kidney and I took a nice little holiday to Cornwall, just the two of us, like a honeymoon. You hear stories about rural bed-and-breakfasts and their conservative owners, but Harbour House didn't mind me sharing a bed with the dead boy.

I walked on the beach and ate ice cream and played a game of mini-golf with myself, which I won spectacularly. I ate fish and chips by the sea and unwillingly fed the seagulls. With the sun still curving lazily to the horizon I returned to my non-judgemental bed and breakfast and made myself a cup of Typhoo.

While I was checking the room for hay, I noticed my phone, still on the nightstand, dead as the dead boy. It died often, now I wasn't calling Mum for half an hour every day with a tube in my belly, and I had stopped patting my pocket to check for it when I went out. Phones are wonderful things, adaptive, like kidneys: the less you use them, the less you need them. The messages I used to receive from guilty friends had dropped off, except on my birthday or when mum sent out one of her emails. They had all stopped except for Jen's. Jen would have kept texting even if she thought I was dead. Perhaps she did.

It took twenty minutes for Mum's texts to finish coming through. GOT JUMPER IN SALE WILL TAKE TO OXFAM IF NO GOOD. HOPE TRAINS OK IN ALL WEEKEND IF U WANT TO CALL. SAW JEN IN TOWN SHE SAYS HELLO. WILL RING WEDS WITH GRAN'S NEW ADDRESS. When I got my diagnosis, she went from keeping her phone down the back of the sofa to texting in her sleep, and she never stopped. Now she kept in near-constant touch just in case I needed anything, and I never called because I couldn't ask her to look after the dead boy the way she had looked after me.

Ten minutes later, while I was pretending to fall asleep in my clothes, the phone beeped again. Jen. *I went to Cornwall when I was 10. A bloke told me he could take me to meet Bob the Builder if I got in his car. Stay safe.* A year ago, that message would have ended *Give me a ring if you're bored* or *Let me know when you're back and I'll take you for a pint*; even Jen had given up on that now. But someone cleverer and better than me made it so that you can get a message like that, press one button, and talk to the person who sent it. So I did.

It took two years for the ringing tone to start. And then:

'Dan! You are literally the last person I was expecting to hear from. I sort of assumed you'd gone off and died without telling anyone.'

'No you didn't. Mum would have told you. Anyway, I've had —'

'Yeah, yeah, I know. We've got other things to talk about than your liver, you know. Have you met her new bloke? He's *ginger*.'

'Look, I'm sorry it's been so long —'

'I've been pining, Dan. Pining.'

'Yeah, I know. I'm in Cornwall.'

'Is that, like, medical slang? Will you be all better when you get to John O'Groats?'

'No, I'm on holiday. Things have been hard. That's why I haven't been in touch. I thought it might help to get away, you know? And I thought while I was at it I should give you a ring.'

'Makes sense. If I was ringing me after this long, I'd want to be two hundred miles away too.'

As I shifted on the bed I realised that I was smiling. A big, tight grin, the kind that ached.

'So how's it all going? You're on the mend at last?'

'I –' I stopped. There was so much to say: I got the surgery; it all went fine; I wasn't dying; I wasn't dying; I wasn't dying. She knew it all, but she deserved to be told it. And I wanted to tell her, but the dead boy had his hand clamped across my mouth. 'I –'

The bedframe creaked as I turned again. The grin was gone but the ache was still there.

'Dan? Can you hear me? I think the signal's going.'

'No, no, it's not that.' I moved my phone from hand to hand while I wiped sweat from palms to bedsheet. 'I –'

'Dan, are you okay?'

A key rattled in the next room's lock. The door scraped open and shut. The dead boy and I said nothing.

'Dan, if you don't speak to me in the next ten seconds, so help me I will drive to Cornwall and I will beat it out of you.'

I closed my eyes and listened to the noise on the line. Four hours and ten seconds later she was there.

It was the longest hug the Padstow Town Car Park had ever seen. Or perhaps it just seemed that way because I was frightened of the beating to follow. When it was over, Jen looked me up and down. 'You look terrible. I didn't think your face could look worse, but you've managed it.'

'I had kidney failure.'

'You can't keep blaming kidney failure for everything. You didn't have face failure, did you? No more than usual.'

I wanted to fight back. Jen had been driving for four hours in her work clothes. She should have been knackered. But she didn't look knackered. She looked wonderful.

'I am knackered,' she said. 'Knackered and starving and sober. Are there any pubs still open?'

I rubbed my disaster of a face. 'To be honest, I haven't been a huge drinker recently,' I said. *But I could be*, I thought, before pushing the thought down very deep indeed.

'Then have cranberry juice, or whatever it is. I've been driving for a fortnight. I'm still trying to drop into neutral whenever I stop moving. I need a drink.'

'I'm not sure they do cranberry juice around here,' I said. 'They think it's a cocktail.'

She shook her head. 'It's no wonder they want to split off, is it? People like you won't get past the border when the revolution comes.'

We settled for the harbour, a floppy pizza, a four-pack of Holsten Pils and a carton of Ocean Spray that Jen insisted on buying for me. We ate and drank and lobbed stones into the sea because we were too high up to skim them. The conversation trundled like I hadn't ignored her texts for eighteen months. Like calling her from an attic room in Cornwall and saying nothing was a perfectly ordinary way to re-establish our friendship. Like I had met the man who was now her fiancé and she had met the part of me that was the dead boy.

We didn't mention hospitals or kidneys until I reminded her about the time she pissed upright at a urinal to prove it could be done and she retorted, 'Yeah, well, at least I've got more than one kidney.'

'Actually,' I said, 'I've got three. They leave the old ones in.'

'Show off.'

Remembering the leaflets and the diagrams, I suddenly had the idea that when I thought I could feel the dead boy's kidney pulling at me, I didn't feel it down near the groin, where they'd put it, but in the small of my back, where my own useless pair sat. Thinking about it there, Jen and I sitting safe on the edge above the black water, I couldn't decide whether it was true.

'Look,' she said, 'do you want to go somewhere a bit less open?'

'No, this is good. It's nice to be out. I've been a bit of a shut-in recently, you know? That's why I came down here, I suppose.'

'To the burgeoning metropolis that is Padstow. Of course. Well, if you're sure. But we should talk, you know? I didn't spend fifty quid on petrol to relive our glory days at the reservoir.'

I looked at her and tried to think about how to start, but instead I thought about kissing her. I don't know why. I didn't want to. But it was strange to think that I could change our whole friendship with such a simple act. Like stepping in front of a train. Would the ring on her finger feel different if she betrayed him? Would it start to weigh on her like the dead boy's kidney weighed on me? They were questions with no answer. Jen had never betrayed anyone in her life.

'I don't like it,' I said. 'The kidney.'

'You don't like your kidney?'

'It's not my kidney. It's some dead kid's. I can feel it in there and I hate it. I hate it. I can't stand it.'

There were a few seconds' silence, and then Jen said: 'You're a fucking idiot, Dan. You're a fucking idiot and you know it.'

If you'd asked me to guess Jen's response, that would have been it, almost to the word. Only I didn't think she'd mean it.

'You've got to sort this out, Dan,' she said. 'You've missed enough of your life already. You can't spend the rest of it moping that your kidney's the wrong colour, and dragging your friends across the country at a moment's notice. It's not fair.' She threw another stone into the sea. 'Look, I'm here for you, you know I am, but I can't help you. I could say maybe you feel guilty that your donor's dead and you're still alive...'

That sounded right. Perhaps that was it.

'... or you got so used to being sick you don't know how to be well any more...'

That sounded right too.

'... or, I don't know, you're just stubborn and you hate that you needed so much help just to stay alive. But it would be bollocks, all of it. Even if it was true. You need a professional, not sea air and a chat. Maybe this is just another side effect and they know all about it. You'll never find out like this.'

I looked at the water. The dead boy had been working hard, trying to get in my good books, and I needed a piss. It would feel good to piss in a great arc over the edge, the light too low to look for blood in the stream. To raise the water level imperceptibly. In the silence, Jen was playing with her engagement ring. I stood, turned a little away, unzipped, and voided.

We drove back the next day, me reading the map, Jen following the satnav. After three hours in the car my back started to hurt, the kind of pain I used to worry was a kidney failing until I was treated to the real thing and it didn't hurt at all. I patted my scar like an obedient dog. Perhaps that was the way I had to start thinking of it: not my kidney, but not the dead boy's either. A scrappy little companion who had survived against the odds. My new best friend. Or second best.

We talked about the wedding, how the original venue had burned down but the new one had a beautiful garden for the reception, how I was going to be a bridesmaid but Jen wouldn't make me wear a dress if I didn't want to. She told me about her fiancé by explaining all the ways he was better than me, starting with his face and ending with his exemplary teetotaller's renal system.

'I'm going to be putting up with kidney jokes from you for the rest of my life, aren't I?' I asked.

'Yes,' she said, 'and you're going to be grateful.'

At the wedding reception, there were hay bales to sit on and it rained and rained and rained. For once, I knew just what I was doing.

'Little Bird Story' is James Collett's second very short story for The Fiction Desk, following 'The Clever Skeleton' in Because of What Happened.

Little Bird Story
James Collett

At the bus depot, early in the morning, the world was turning in a funny way. It was a summer day, but early enough to be cold. It was one of those bus depots where there isn't anything but traffic noise and gravel and wind and a toilet block that's always locked. My hangover was bad and things generally were bad.

I was waiting for an early Megabus to see someone I hadn't seen for a while, because I wanted to show her that I did sober-person things, like taking the earliest bus on the timetable. I was pretending to everyone that everything was all right now.

I'd been drinking more because of all the lying. My bones were sharp inside me. I felt filthy, and jagged as a mangled can. Each time I moved, it seemed I hurt someone I did not wish to hurt. Every day, I woke up afraid of what had happened and what I'd done. There was always a shameful thing. Always I'd borrowed or stolen or lied or somehow blundered, but especially I had always lied: 'No, I hardly drink at all now. Couple of beers a night.' I always remembered the lies and realised that I had not really been believed.

It was all for nothing, I thought. I walked round to the other side of the toilet block to be away from the other people at the depot. The block had a kind of anteroom, with timetables and a few seats, but the whole block was locked up and you couldn't get into the anteroom or the toilets. You could see into the anteroom, though, through a large window. I stood beside the window and rolled a cigarette. I was too hungover to smoke, but I tried. I took very small, sucking drags and exhaled quickly.

I'd always thought that nothing happened at bus depots; you just waited and felt ugly, or felt pretty, depending on who you were. But at the window that morning, something really happened, right next to my head, without warning or calculation. The sound of it shuddered, horrible and hard, in the middle of me, because I knew that the tiny yellow flash and loud bang and small, sad crunch meant that a songbird had flown into the window and that the songbird would be dead; ripped from its flight and its life by a senseless bus depot toilet block window.

It was a goldcrest, the size of a ping-pong ball, and it dropped, flapped it wings once on the ground; then it just lay there on its back, looking very small. For a few seconds, I felt the panic of responsibility and I didn't know what to do. I dropped my roll-up and my hands began to shake. I scratched my head and felt stupid.

I remembered someone telling me that birds always die if left on their backs, and I thought I'd give the goldcrest a chance. I cupped my hand underneath it and felt that it was twitching a little. I turned it over and backed away a few steps, but it had stopped moving. It lay on its belly with its wings floppy and lifeless. Its face was limp on the tarmac, its beak turned to one side underneath it; a smashed little bird with yellow feathers and legs as thin as needles. I kicked the wall of the toilet block and shouted some dirty things. A group of young Japanese girls, who'd just walked to my side of the block, abruptly stopped chattering and turned around.

I made a new cigarette and walked up and down, thinking about how heavy and unpleasant humans were. I went back to the goldcrest and it still wasn't moving. I crouched over it and gently prodded its tail. It shifted forward, fractionally: its legs must have moved. I thought the movement might have just been a flicker of dead nerves, a tiny death throe, and at first it made me even sadder. But then the bird lifted its head.

It straightened its neck so that its beak faced forward instead of to the side. Very slowly, its feathers ruffled and its head rose higher. After a few minutes, it got to its feet and swayed, all punch-drunk. It looked around itself, staggering a bit, and moved its wings in a way that made it look like it was shrugging its shoulders. It was getting its little head together, I suppose.

Suddenly it flew up to the top of a fence post, where it further composed itself and dusted itself down. Then I knew it was all right.

The bus arrived and I got on. I had a bottle of port in my bag (it wasn't really port – ssshhhhh – it was very cheap and I didn't know what it really was), and I took a seat and had a good drink. You weren't allowed to drink on the Megabus and I was kicked off a couple of miles along the road. The other people on the Megabus looked at me sternly and thought I was a nuisance, but I didn't mind. I knew it was all right.

Peter Clarke is making his Fiction Desk debut with this story of escapism and addiction. Do bear in mind that the following story is a work of fiction, and you shouldn't actually do what he tells you.

Constructing an Exit
Peter Clarke

First, have asthma. This is a prerequisite for everything that follows. Being born with it is the easiest route for everyone; just make sure you don't grow out of it too soon (some people do) or you'll waste the opportunity.

If you're worried, there are things you can do to help stay short of breath. Go camping. Why not? Sit by campfires breathing in deeply. Or else start hanging out with your dad in the garage more often. Watch him dismantle his scramblers, ask questions. Get closer — as close as he'll let you, with all that rusted metal strewn around. Now breathe. Follow the line of smoke from the tip of his roll-up. Try to catch it without him noticing.

Let your old man tell you how he came off his bike straight into a tree one time; how another time he ended up hanging from barbed wire seven feet in the air and had to be cut down by four other blokes on the same outing. You've heard it all before, but it helps if you can make the right noises in the right places anyway. Lean in close, breathe the smoke once he's done with it. Ignore your mum calling you until the last possible moment. Or don't. Go inside, do whatever it is she wants you to do (set the table, put the PlayStation controllers away), and come back out to the garage. Your dad will shake his head, light another ciggie from a line of already-rolled ones he keeps on the side.

Maybe you steal a rollie and try smoking for yourself. Or maybe you don't.

If the above doesn't do the trick, if all that smoke doesn't keep the asthma at a steady peak, wait until the summer, go out and stand in a field or allotment. Anywhere you can find where there might be a high pollen count. Stand there and breathe. Yes. *Breathe*. Lose the hay fever medication and go it alone. That might help.

Be imaginative, be creative. Try and try again. Whatever your approach, you'll get there if you want it enough (and you do want it, believe me).

When you're wheezing properly you'll be ready — and when you're ready, read on.

There are some other things you'll need too. A doctor, for instance, is vital. Also someone to take you to appointments and pick up prescriptions for you (you can't drive yourself, kid). Also an impulse towards idiocy, or lack of forethought, or an almost psychopathic inability to track the consequences of your own choices; whichever suits.

An addictive or obsessive personality is not essential, but if you think you have one by this point then fine, go with that. It will at least give you an excuse to fall back on when you need it later. Self-justification can be tricky sometimes. You'll find that out soon enough.

If you don't have an addictive personality, or you don't think you do... well, don't worry about it. It's not an issue. You're still a minor after all. You don't need excuses just yet. You're not old enough to know any better.

Start slowly. You need to learn how to use something properly before you can start to mess with it. Remember how you learned to read aloud, remember the kah-ah-tuh, the phonetic cat? You have to learn the principles, learn the components, and then you're well away. It's all a learning curve. It'll be worth it though, in the end.

Listen to the doctors and nurses. They're trying to help, that's all — and they will help, eventually, although maybe not in the way they're expecting to. Take in what they tell you. It's important. Try not to be too distracted by the long wait, the strong smell of witch hazel in those tiny box rooms.

Study the doctor's face, or the nurse's. Watch them. Your first doctor looks like a headmaster you'll have later on in secondary school. The first nurse you meet looks like one of your mum's friends in photographs from before your parents were married. She's smiling though. It's okay. It's not difficult what they're asking you to do. Not yet, anyway.

Look. Listen. Take it in.

This is what you need to do:

The blue one is the reliever. This is the one you take when you're feeling wheezy or out of breath. It will help you to breathe easily again. Take two puffs; we'll show you how.

The brown one is a little different from the blue one. The brown one is the preventer. It helps your airways stay open and stops you from feeling wheezy in the first place, so that you shouldn't need to take the blue one. Okay? You don't need to be wheezy to take the brown one. That's important. Take two puffs in the morning after you wake up and two more at night before you go to sleep. Make sure that you always leave thirty seconds between each puff to give your lungs time to absorb the medicine.

To take a puff, first shake the inhaler. Then breathe out, counting to five. Then put the inhaler in your mouth. That's right. Start to breathe in, then push the top of the inhaler down – do it hard. Keep breathing in for as long as you can. Steadily, steadily. Then take the inhaler out of your mouth and breathe out. Okay?

To take the second puff, all you need to do is repeat what you've just done. Take a puff. Wait thirty seconds. Then repeat the same steps for the second puff. Okay?

Do you see, champ?

Did you get that, love?

Always read the enclosed leaflet carefully. Always use your inhaler exactly as your doctor has told you to. Do not exceed the stated dose.

Give yourself some time. You'll need to practise, to get the hang of what exactly is expected of you. It could take years. Things will change.

You'll move house twice. You'll have to share a bedroom with your sister for a while. You'll make new friends at new schools. You'll have a couple of accidents, break bones (but they'll heal). You'll fall down the stairs and break your arm, chip a tooth on the skirting board where the stairs turn for the last three steps to the hall. You'll leave a dent, a gouge in the paint that will still be there when you move out. Maybe you're pushed or maybe you're just clumsy. Only your sister will ever know the truth on that one.

You'll go over the handlebars of your bike at the skate park and give yourself a concussion (good work). Probably, you'll get into a fight or two with some of the other kids. They make fun of you when you're wheezy and vulnerable. *Darth Inhaler! Darth Inhaler!* You might shrug it off. You might play up to it *(I find my lack of breath disturbing...).* Or you might not, depending on how you're feeling at the time. There could be fights. It's a possibility. Just try not to break anything else. You'll spend enough time at the doctor's as it is. Trust me. You'll need to go for asthma check-ups, for a start. The doctors insist.

At these check-ups, the doctor or nurse will ask you to blow into a cardboard tube so that they can measure the capacity of your lungs. This is called a Peak Flow Test. You won't pass. Remember that you can't breathe all that well. Be patient (no pun intended). Take a deep, calming breath (sorry). Now go for it. That's it. Give it everything.

The doctor or nurse might ask you to take the test a few times, to compare results. Breathe in for as long as you can, take a moment, then let it all out. Or try the rocket method, taking your breath in slowly, letting it out again in one quick puff. Or just puff your cheeks a little and get straight to it. Try not to worry if you don't get any better. They will stop asking after two or three tries. The cardboard tube will go in the hazardous waste bin and you can put this behind you, move on.

The doctor or nurse will ask you some questions about your asthma too. Tell the truth, or mostly the truth. If you've forgotten to take the brown one for two weeks (you will, at one point), this is probably the kind of thing you're better off not mentioning.

They might ask, *Do you have difficulties in any aspect of your life as a direct result of being asthmatic?* Sounds like an essay question, doesn't it? But this is the kind of thing they ask sometimes. If your parents are there, now might be the time to look at them.

I... don't... think... so.

Depending on how diligent the doctor/nurse is, they might also ask you to show them how you take your inhalers. They'll get out another cardboard tube and a fake inhaler that's about twice the size of the one you carry. Either that or they'll ask you to get your own inhaler out and they'll have you use that — without (and this is crucial) actually taking it.

Show them how you shake the inhaler, breathe out, put the inhaler in your mouth, breath in, push the top down hard (or don't!) and keep breathing in to the maximum capacity of your poor, damaged lungs. Show them the pause between puffs. This will probably be much longer than you actually pause. But still: show them. Count using Mississippis or Locomotives or Elephants or whatever.

How long was that?

Eventually, mime taking the second puff. The doctor/nurse, if they have nothing else to say, will probably tell you that you didn't wait long enough.

Keep going. Give yourself a little longer. Live. Mutter pep-talks to yourself on the way to school (or don't). Take your inhalers exactly as your doctor told you to (or don't). Carry on, day by day. Then stop.

Pick a day, any day. There might be a trigger and there might not. A trigger, if there is one, can be anything. An argument with your sister that results in your bedroom door being pulled off its hinges. Someone you thought was a friend using you to practise his one-inch punch in the driveway of your mum's friend's house. Your dad losing his job. Your sister getting kidnapped. Your maths homework. Anything. Real or imaginary, fact or fiction.

Pick a day, a time, a trigger. Then ask yourself, one last decision: which one will it be? Blue? Or brown? Make your choice. Don't worry, you don't have to stick to it after this (and you won't). You just have to make it. Now. Do it now.

Did you make it? Which one did you pick?

Here it is, then. The first time. Take a puff, wait a second, take another puff, wait a second, take another puff, wait, take another puff, wait, take another puff. And another puff, and another, and another. How many was that? Eight. Okay.

Now wait.

You sit on the edge of your unmade bed, in your bedroom, alone. You lie down on the carpet. Focus on your chest, your heart. Picture your alveoli, your red blood cells. Picture your heart valves open and closing, expanding and contracting. Follow a swirl of paint on the ceiling. Your heart is pounding but your lungs are calm.

There might be a faint haze of colour at the edge of your vision, but what colour is it, exactly — indigo, violet?

Don't worry if you don't see a colour straight away. It won't always be the same. The colour will come later, or it won't come at all and something else will.

For now, put the inhaler down. Remember to breathe. You still need to breathe. Close your eyes and concentrate. Open your eyes. Look around you from here, from your place on the floor. What do you see? Speak now, don't think. You can't overthink this. Just say the first thing that comes into your head.

How do you feel?

Okay, so. Once. Good.

Well, not good, but okay.

Well, not okay, but not bad.

You were just experimenting, just seeing what would happen.

You just needed a bigger dose, just that once, and you won't try it again.

Think of the hospital dramas you've seen on TV. *Casualty*. *Holby City*. Think about pain medication, how it works, how people develop a tolerance the longer they're on a particular medicine and need a bigger dose to have the same effect.

Think of your terrible Peak Flow results and wonder if you'd be able to do any better now.

Or else don't think anything at all. It doesn't matter. It's your choice.

But there are things you can tell yourself, there are plenty of excuses for this type of behaviour, if you need them.

The next time, you're at school.

Bored of sports, you and your friends have had to find something else to do with yourselves at break times. Last year it was Pogs and British Bulldog. But Pogs got boring (nobody played properly anyway) and British Bulldog was banned by the headmaster after a kid tripped crossing the safety line and dislocated his jaw.

You are in year five or year six. You will be out of there soon and up to secondary school. In the meantime, you need something to keep you occupied.

Mostly, you go behind the mound at the bottom of the playing field and scrap. Five-a-side skirmishes, tactical fights, impromptu bundles. You spend much of your lunchtimes listening out, on edge. If someone decides to shout *Scrap!* you don't want to be the last guy to react. You've been at the bottom of a bundle before and don't much fancy doing it again. It stinks, for a start. Farts and BO.

Sometimes maybe you sneak into the nature reserve to hunt for snakes you're pretty sure don't exist, or else to see if you can find your way through to the gap in the fence on the other side, which everybody knows leads through to a park you can't get to any other way.

Sometimes maybe you all stand on either side of the pond, out of sight, and throw pebbles at each other, just because.

More recently, you've come up with something new, something exciting. How it works is: you get one of the big guys to spin another guy around by the arms and let go, so that he goes flying — dizzily, spastically — across the playing field. You wait for him to fall, to lose his balance and go over, and you cheer.

That's it. It's that simple. Points are scored for how long someone is able to stay on their feet after they're thrown. Ten bonus points are up for grabs for anyone who doesn't go down at all. There is a score table where tallies are kept. You drew it, that first day, over two pages at the back of your history book.

One of your friends is bound to have a G-shock watch with a timer built in. Maybe you all have one. You can take it in turns to time, maybe, and someone else can record the scores. You'll have daily tournaments, weekly totals. The winner gets... what? Fame and glory. Chocolate cigarettes. A half-finished bottle of Coke. Someone else's sandwiches. It's not a lot, but there's not much any of you can afford to give the others, not on your pocket money.

When it's your turn to spin, hold out your arms. Let the guy take your wrists, let him spin you, let him let you go. The feeling, near flight, is similar to the feeling you got on your bedroom floor that one time. Breath tightening, blood loosening, lungs expanding, heart pumping. In your mind's eye you see a train speeding along the tracks. You see an elastic band from a half-remembered physics experiment, twisting tighter and tighter before it is let go and pings off into the distance, never to be found.

Except maybe the field has been mown recently, maybe your breath comes suddenly short. This wasn't part of the plan. You come to a halt sprawled on the grass of the mound and you think you're about to have an asthma attack. Now. With everyone watching.

Try to think of the last time you had an attack, if you can remember it. What did you do then? Two puffs. A deep, catching breath. Another two puffs.

Come on, come on. Do something. Work.

You feel the cold sting of the spray propellant in the back of your throat. There's a whirring in front of your eyes which might, or might not, be related to the spinning and flinging.

Stand up, or try to. Only ten seconds on your feet this time. A rubbish attempt. Absolute rubbish. But your friends have spotted the inhaler and they let you off. Darth Inhaler isn't much of a problem for you anymore.

You okay? they ask, coming over. *Are you okay?*

Take another two puffs, breathing in until your lungs hit that too-familiar wall. Nod hesitantly, the inhaler still in your mouth, your eyes wide from a combination of the near-miss attack and the medicine now working its way into your lungs. Your world is spinning. But: *I'm all right*, you say. *I'm okay, I'm okay.*

And you are. Of course you are.

How many puffs was that?

Your mum, calling from the kitchen.

Startled, you thrust the inhaler into your pocket without its cap. *Two*, you call back. The cap is on the windowsill beside your dad's murky shaving mirror. Pick it up. Think. It didn't work properly the first couple of puffs. Go on: say it. But you haven't been paying attention. You might already have said that, you don't know, you're not sure. When you thought it, did the words fall out of your mouth or didn't they? Think.

The colourful haze surrounding your vision seems to be spreading, changing.

Shut your eyes. Get rid of it. But the image of the shower cubicle in front of you stays right where it was, flickering slightly. The pattern of duct tape where your sister punched it when the water wouldn't run hot one Saturday morning. Trace it with your fingers. Pick at the edges of the thick grey tape.

In the kitchen, your mum makes a *Humph* noise, loud enough for you to hear. Nothing else after that, though. You're in the clear, but barely. Breathe. Reach for the key and turn it and step out of the bathroom. Back to *Tekken 2*. The final boss, where Kazuya turns into a devil and starts spraying fire.

Make a note: You will need to be more careful than this.

Give it some time. Days, weeks, a month.

One day, in a stroke of inspiration, you will come up with something new for those sometimes-still-boring lunchtimes. Think about it. Two guys on either side of the playing field, spinning two other guys, flinging both guys at the same time (there will need to be someone to count them in) so that they whirl haphazardly, heads down, eyes closed, waiting for contact. There will be a hardcore version too, played on concrete rather than grass and in full view of the staff room window. There will be moves called the windmill, the combine-harvester, the rake. Farmyard imagery, nobody knows why. Another move, from WWF wrestling, is called the clothesline. A flurry of fists and feet. A dizzy mess.

Go on. Be brave, volunteer. Be a guinea pig for your own invention, it's the only way. Feel the pressure on your wrists, fingerprint bruises that will form later in the day. Hold your breath. Spin. Feel your legs careering beneath you as you're let go.

Feel the sun and the breeze on your face. In front of your eyes, a blur of colour and movement. Are you ready? Better hope so, because it's too late if not, you should have said something earlier. This is it now. This is happening.

Clench your fists. Flail. Here he comes now. Here he comes: the other guy.

Are you ready?

Then, three days into a cottage holiday in the Lake District with your grandparents, you are lying on a plastic-covered, pee-proof mattress, head on one of the two hypoallergenic pillows your mum insisted you bring with you, running your tongue over your teeth, while in your head, or rather hovering in front of your eyes, there's an image, a cartoon version of your tongue wearing a dusty brown ten-gallon hat, speeding past teeth too white to have anything to do with yours. Noise of the wind rushing by in your ears, a pounding on the left side of your chest and music rising: *ten-to-ten-to-ten-to-ten-to-ten.*

Cowboy time!

Your sister is asleep across the room, snoring at the wall. You smile, or think you do, but then your tongue does a full revolution of your mouth and you can feel it, twisted and caught. That's not right, is it; it shouldn't do that! You cough and heave, bucking on the bed like the plastic donkey in that game you used to play together.

With a start, your sister wakes up. *What? What is it?*
Cowboy time! you say. *Buck, buck, buckaroo!*
Maybe she looks at you, or maybe she doesn't.
A minute passes. An hour.
Maybe you don't choke, maybe you don't say anything. Maybe you just lie there, buzzing. Maybe your sister doesn't wake up at all.

You throw an empty inhaler in the bin in three pieces: the canister, the cap, the shell.

Push the pieces to the bottom of the bin, arrange some used tissues over them, then cover the tissues with the plastic tray from some chicken fillets. Bury the pieces in a pile of leaves in the park on the way home from school. Throw them in a dog-poo bin with your unwanted, uneaten ham sandwiches.

Or maybe your sister comes in from the garden and you lob the inhaler into a nearby utility-room cupboard. Open the cupboard door, throw the inhaler in, close the door again quick-sharp. Pretend that the empty inhaler is a smoke grenade you're throwing into a building full of terrorists.

You will get good at this. Hiding, thinking on your feet. You might not think so straight away, but you will do. Eventually.

There are two hundred metred actuations in one inhaler. Six puffs, eight, sixteen, twenty-two, thirty-six. You go through an inhaler in a week and get rid of it. Perhaps you drop it down the drain. It's an option. Five days. Six. You're not counting. Not properly.

At two puffs maybe five days a week it used to take twenty weeks to empty a blue inhaler. Four puffs a day for the brown one would last you fifty days, seven weeks. But don't worry about that. Try not to think about it now. There are three more blue and two more brown in the bathroom cupboard after all: a neat stack of rectangular boxes, prescription stickers folded across the side, your name on every one of them.

Okay. Now describe it. Or try to. The buzz, the whirr, the whirling, the spiral. Trust your gut, trust your instincts, just this once. You need to trust me, kid.

Try to think about it in comparison, in metaphors and similes. That feeling that moves from one side of your chest to the other, what is that? A tightening, an elastic band ball like the one your mum has on her desk in the study, bouncing. No, not bouncing, twisting. A single elastic band removed from the ball, twisting tighter and tighter and pinging off. Rainbow lines around the edges of your vision, blurred as if seen through mist. Your movement becomes robotic — if you even move at all.

Once or twice you have found yourself rooted to the ground: an oak tree, or else a beech, tall and impervious, *I shall not be moved!* Looking down, you saw roots pushing through the carpet. Actual rips in the actual carpet, no matter that you were upstairs at the time and should have fallen straight through. The underlay was puckered around you. Once or twice or three times, maybe.

More often, you just stare, cherishing the feeling, the release. You are as blank as a summer sky, as the new whiteboards that were delivered to your school last year. Stare for long enough and something seems to click into place. The world tilts and opens. You are no longer blinking or breathing. You don't need to worry about any of that stuff anymore. You tingle. You twang. You are a taut rope, a stretched piece of string.

Remember: *How long's dinner going to be?* you used to ask, and your dad would put his fingers on the table in front of him. *About this long*, he'd say.

There is an intermittent feeling of falling. And there is a door in front of you, this crack in the world. Ask yourself, *When is a door not a door? How does an entrance become an exit?*

Remember: Once you reached out a hand towards that crack and touched... nothing. Air. Nitrogen and oxygen and argon and carbon dioxide. Trace gases — probably more than a hint of the drugs you've been taking. Betamethasone dipropionate. Salbutamol sulphate. The CFC-free propellants. You touched all of this and yet you felt... nothing... A few seconds passed before you realised you couldn't feel your arm, even though you could clearly see it stretching from your trunk in front of you. No more feeling. No more falling. You closed your eyes and when you opened them you were still standing there on tired twigs, looking out of your bedroom window at the darkness outside.

How long had you been standing there, while your family and friends and the rest of the world carried on around you? You didn't know. An hour? A day? You were the Tardis — the *Retardis*. For just a little while, you were moving through time. You were two feet away from the world and one storey above it behind double glazing, with your eyes closed and your arms at your side, in the dark, alone. You were there. Maybe you are there even now.

This is how it feels, then, to remove your self from yourself. This is how it feels to have one foot in the real world, to be here and not-here, in place, but apart. Remember this (you will): It is nice to get away.

This new story from Sarah Evans demonstrates that when it comes to crowdfunding, the sky's the limit. The sky, and no further.

Misson to Mars: An A–Z Guide

Sarah Evans

A is for apple, the longing to sink teeth into crisp fresh produce.
   A is for arsenic, a component of Martian soil.
   A is for airlocks, adventure and applicants, over two hundred thousand of us whittled down. See also F - Forty.
   A is for abandoned and alone.

B is for blue, the colour of home, for bravery and bravado.
   B is for business plan, badly conceived, badly gone wrong. See also C - Crowdfunding.

C is for calcium, leeching out of bones, slowly reducing any possibility of return. C is for crowdfunding, unreliable as it happens. See also Y.

C is for cosmic radiation, colonisation and commitment. C is for comms links, cameras, and cutting them off.

D is for daydreams, for dreamers, for derring-do and diminishing supplies. D is for drinking water of the recycled and reclaimed kind. See also W - Water. D is for understanding the deal.

D is for dying, one by one.

E is for Earth, a small blue dot, visible at certain times in the morning sky. E is for enterprise - private. See also B - Business plan. E is for eight years.

F is for funding and for failure. F is for faith (see also K - Keeping), fate, and fortune. F is for forty, the number of us chosen, and for future generations, those who will follow in our footsteps, but who come too late. F is for followers, as in 'social media', as in 'too few'.

G is for 38% gravity. See also C - Calcium. G is for grave.

H is for the heroes that we all believed we'd become. H is for the home left behind and for habitat unit (Martian).

H is for help, as in 'cry for'. H is for hope, diminished, but not extinguished.

I is for I, as in 'unimportant'. See also W - We. I is for individual, as in 'the project is bigger than any one'. I is for isolation, intrepidity, and indifference.

I is for sheer fucking idiocy.

J is for joke, a bad one and on us; for journalists and the fickleness of their interest. J is for journey, a long one.

K is for killer idea. K is for keeping, as in 'faith,' 'spirits up,' and 'our side of the bargain.'

L is for lottery, the one in a million chance of being chosen and we all thought we were the lucky ones. See also O – Odds.
  L is for lethal hazards, laboratory, long duration, and longing.
  L is for lonely, the utter aloneness of a handful of people, so very far from home.

M is for Mars, our lonely outpost. M is for mission.
  M is for Martian dust, potentially (and in fact) toxic. M is for mission control, and its ineptitude.
  M is for Martian habitat unit, Martian rover, Martian water etc, etc, and for all the things we miss.
  M is for madness and mission to Mars.

N is for no, ne, nie, nee, nein, non, nej, nahi, nem, nai, naa, não, nu, niet, noon. As in 'this cannot be happening.' As in 'response to our distress call'. See also H – Help, cry for. N is for nausea caused by: low gravity, arsenic, panic.

O is for oxygen, one of several vital things in short supply. O is for once in a lifetime opportunity. O is for the low odds of this mission ever being a success, but we understood the risks and plunged ahead anyway. O is for over and out.

P is for please and pleading, and our cries falling on deaf ears. P is for pioneers and for planet, as in 'red'. P is for psychological and sociological profiling, the endless tests we got through, meaning we are better able to cope with the current bleak outlook than most people would be, which is some (not much) consolation. P is for public funding, as in 'none'. P is for playing to the camera, to no avail.

P is for past and present, but not for future.

Q is for questions. See also Y.

R is for the red dusty landscape, for robotic explorers (not quite up to the job of water extraction) and for radiation (inadequate protection from). R is for risk, for rescue and its diminishing likelihood.

S is for survivors, our slowly fading numbers. S is for space, space travel, spacecraft etc, etc. S is for stars and stargazing. S is for self-sustainability (insufficient), for supplies (dwindling), support systems and support being withdrawn. S is for suiting-up, surface explorations, solar flares and storm shelters.

S is for six months, the time it would take even the fastest of rockets to arrive.

S is for stranded.

T is for trouble, as in 'getting into with no way out', and for trusting, as in 'overly'. T is for training, as in eight earth years.

U is for us. See also W – We.

V is for viewer numbers and the way they fell away. V is for the vastness of space. V is for viability (or not) and vision (misguided).

W is for we, as in 'plural pronoun', as in 'not I'. W is for water, recycled plus recovered from planet surface, which have jointly proved not enough.

X is for x-ray and more general radiation, the type that will kill you, but only slowly. X is for that X factor, the stars we were destined to become.

Y is for why?

Y we chose to do this. Y we trusted that an audacious mission to colonise Mars could be funded privately via crowdfunding plus TV rights for 24/7 footage. Y such footage has failed to generate sufficient cashflow. See also C – Cameras, Comms links, Cut off.

Y the mission failed.

Z is for zero-gravity, zero-liability clauses, zero-accountability.

Z is for Zeitgeist, for misjudging the spirit of our time.

Z is for zeds, sleep without end, the type that will take us in succession, until a lone individual remains, until that final pioneer reaches their limit.

Z is for zero.

This slice of science fiction from Edmund Krikorian is a reminder that the big stories and the little stories get tangled up together. It's also timely: just as we go to press, there is news that the wreck of the original Santa Maria may have been found off the coast of Haiti.

Santa Maria
Edmund Krikorian

School today was boring as ever. My desk is right at the back of the class and to the far left. It's easy to make yourself unnoticeable. The teachers barely ask me anything anymore. The best thing is that I can stare at Hannah and nobody can see me doing it.

When I first arrived, everyone wanted to know me because Jimbo is my uncle. Even though it has only been six or so months since we left, the cliques have already formed and I'm not really in any of them. I'm not one of the losers, but I'm also not one of the cool kids. That's okay. Being a cool kid looks hard. Every few weeks one of them falls out with the others and gets ostracised. Henry was like that. Now he sits next to me and chews his nails and looks like he doesn't sleep enough. I avoid him.

Anyway, no one really got any work done today, because Uncle Jim is visiting tomorrow to talk to us and everyone's too excited to concentrate. We all just wanted the day to end so that the next one would come. Uncle Jim is governor of the ship, and he's the most awesome guy I know. He's really big and his voice fills a room. Even though he's got loads to do, he still finds time to talk to people. He's always laughing. In fact, when he comes to talk to the school, I'll definitely get some kudos points. Hopefully he'll come over and talk to me. Hopefully Freddie and Will and the other cool kids will see. Hopefully Hannah will see too.

I usually hang out with Phil in breaktimes. Phil's quiet and maybe one rung down the social ladder than me, but he's a mate and it's good to have at least one friend that you can rely on. Today we sit on the fence and talk about what we'd do if we had superpowers. I tell him I'd be telekinetic, and I'd go round fighting crime. Phil says what crime, there isn't any crime on this ship. He's right. It's hard to be a hero in a place where there's barely two thousand people. There are too many connections; any criminal would be caught instantly. Besides, nobody really has much that others don't have. All our flats are the same, all our food is the same. Phil says he'd be able to read minds, then he'd know what girls are thinking and how to have ess eee ex with them. I laugh at the image of Phil, with a goatee beard, mindreading the girls in our class. As I laugh, I wonder whether being a mindreader would help with Hannah. I don't know how to make her notice me.

After school I generally like to walk back the long way, on Einstein Walk. Einstein definitely lucked out, his road is by far the nicest. It's where the great windows are, so as I walk back to the resblock I gaze out into space. Vast blackness studded with points of shimmering light. When I was younger this used to terrify me. I worried that the glass would break, that I'd be sucked into space and drift until my lungs gave out and I choked and died, alone in space. Or I'd get pulled by gravity into a star and my body would burn at millions of degrees while I screamed. Dad told me that this wouldn't happen; he said that it wasn't glass the windows were made out of, but something harder than diamond. But he didn't sound reassuring. Uncle Jim clapped me on the back and told me not to be wet. That didn't really help either. I think it was because I was young and babyish. Now that I'm almost eleven, I like to come this way and lose a few minutes staring. It no longer scares me.

Today I got back to our flat in the resblock, same as everyone else's, and grabbed a bagmeal from the storage. I can't really remember what food tasted like on Earth, but sometimes, when I eat a bagmeal, I feel cheated and I don't know why. Dad complains about it the whole time. He doesn't ever do anything about it, he just complains. He always says that we should have had more cows and chickens rather than the vast synthetic farm that's always whirring at the back of the ship. But Uncle Jim says that it would never have worked, that we are part of something incredible and that we should all pull together to make sure it works. He says if making history means having a bland meal, then so be it.

Dad was there when I got back today, asked me about school (even though I don't think he actually cares and I always say the same thing anyway: 'was okay'). Then we sat together at the table in silence and ate our bagmeals, Dad making a face whenever he chewed a lump of meat. He doesn't talk much. Sometimes I feel sorry for him, because I'm sure that he's trying to be closer to me after Mum died. But he always seems... weak. Occasionally I catch myself wishing that Mum were still here instead of him. When that happens I push the thought out of my head, because I hate it and I hate myself for thinking it. But it still comes back.

Supper is usually the only time that Dad and I hang out. I went to my room afterwards and did my homework. The artificial sun is always dimmer at this point, so I put on my desk lamp and worked at the tiny desk in my room. Then I showered, did my teeth, and went to bed. I lay there and thought of tomorrow. Tomorrow is an opportunity. An opportunity to win respect. Maybe more. I drifted off thinking of rescuing Hannah from a great fire, carrying her out of a burning resblock, feeling the skin of her arms around my neck, her head on my shoulder.

I woke today with a tingling in my stomach. The morning routine flew past. I was anxious to get there so I took the straight route, on Hawking Road. I think we're meant to be learning about him in school soon. Everyone was milling outside, waiting for the bell to go. You could feel a buzz about the place. Even the teachers looked as though they'd made an effort. Well, some of them at least.

The bell went, and we all filed in for assembly. Uncle Jim was there! He was standing on the platform at the front of the assembly hall. I tried to catch his eye but he didn't see me.

The head came in, and droned on about how we had a very special guest come to speak to us, and introduced Uncle Jim. Uncle Jim thanked him and took centre stage. He really is massive; next to him the head, who usually seems so fierce, seemed weak and small. Uncle Jim looked us all over for a minute. Then he winked at the whole room.

'Hi everyone! It's great to be here with all of you.' His voice filled the room. 'I've been meaning to come and talk to you all for some time now, but I haven't had the opportunity. It's been busy!' Everyone laughed. Uncle Jim didn't actually have to be all that funny to make people laugh: you could just sense when you were meant to be laughing and so you would.

'The reason I've been meaning to talk to you is a simple one. You are, without doubt...' he paused for a moment, 'the most important people on this ship!

'I know it might not seem that way to you. It probably doesn't seem that way when you're doing homework, am I right?' Of course he was. More laughter. 'But in fact it's true. It's true because you are the legacy. You are the next generation. Each of you is going to play a crucial role in this ship's destiny.

'You are great, great kids. As this magnificent triumph of science and engineering rolls on through space, I encourage you to contemplate the future. Cast your minds hundreds of years ahead, when your children's children step out onto a new world. A new Earth. A new planet for humanity.'

Uncle Jim paused. I looked around. Everyone was spellbound. I felt a burst of pride.

'You are nothing less than the future of mankind!'

Everyone applauded. Some of the older girls wiped away tears in a conspicuous fashion. I glanced over at Hannah, who was in the same row as me. She was laughing and clapping along with everyone else.

The head shook hands with Uncle Jim, and took centre stage. 'Thank you very much to Jim Macht for giving us some of his very valuable time. Classes will now begin as normal, so form your lines.'

My heart plummeted as I saw that Uncle Jim was clearly about to leave. He pulled out his phone, frowned at something that he saw on it, and left without a glance backwards. He hadn't come to talk to me. He hadn't even acknowledged me. I saw Hannah ahead of me in the line. She was talking to Freddie, cool Freddie, king of the class Freddie, and giggling. I felt my heart lurch, while helpless, hot shame washed over me.

Morning classes dragged by today. I tried to daydream about what might have been but my dreams were soured by the present. For a while I found a kind of miserable happiness in daydreaming about my own death, with Hannah crying at my coffin and Uncle Jim looking shocked and sad. That'd show them.

Dad was on the phone when I got home. I could tell it was political stuff because he had his self-righteous tone on. He sometimes uses it when getting me to do stuff I don't actually want to do, but that is somehow 'good' for me. I tuned out, although I kept catching the odd phrase like 'Citizens' Committee' or 'Democratic Rights.' I know what democracy is because we were taught it in school. Everyone gets a vote on things. Uncle Jim says it's a lofty ideal but in practice everyone elects one person to tell them what to do. I don't know what a lofty ideal is, but I can tell that Dad is full of lofty ideals. When he's not trying to 'connect' with me, that is. I wish he wouldn't, it just makes me feel awkward.

Dad seems angry on the phone. I wonder if it's about the cadet training again. The one newspaper that we have on this ship, 'The Santa Maria Daily', carried this story a week ago and Dad just blew up. I couldn't really see what the big deal was, but Dad starting hamming on about martial law and a slippery slope and the tip of an iceberg and I just tuned out. The law's some requirement that us children should have cadet classes and learn about army stuff like marching and camping and stuff. Uncle Jim said in the paper that it was crucial to have discipline on a ship like this, where our lives depend on ship maintenance and order.

Dad and Uncle Jim are brothers, but they don't get on. That's why Uncle Jim never visits. I wish my dad would make more of an effort, but every time I bring it up he goes off on one. It's embarrassing. That's why I always resist when he offers to pick me up at the school gates. I think that Dad might be jealous of the fact that Uncle Jim is governor and gets on really well with all the engineers, whereas Dad is just a legal advisor and doesn't really have much of a role here given that people don't fight much.

Anyway, the cadet training sounds fun. We'd get to march, and dress up like an army, and camp in the massive central gardens (although that seems kind of pointless given that our beds in the resblocks would be about five minutes away). I hope it goes through and we get to do it.

Everyone at school today was talking about the cadet training and how cool it'd be. Ben's brother Jake (who's in the top year) told us in break that the top years would get to learn how to use guns. Henry said that there weren't any guns on the ship. That surprised me because Henry doesn't say much these days. Jake looked contemptuous and said that of course there were guns, but they were secret. 'What would happen if there was a revolt? You think Jimbo would have sanctioned take-off without guns? Mong.' Henry just went back to chewing his nails and saying nothing. Everyone was sucking up to Jake, but I thought that you couldn't be very cool if you were stuck talking to the lower years.

It all got pushed out my head when I saw Freddie pass a note to Steve who passed it to Rachel who passed it to Hannah, who giggled behind her hand and was smiling through the rest of double maths. I spent the rest of the lesson doodling elaborate torture devices that I would use on Freddie, then scribbling them out in case anyone saw.

Hannah is really lovely. She has golden hair and it's all straight like the older girls'. She has a few light freckles and bright blue eyes. She's really cool and other girls all flock round her, like iron filings to a magnet. I've never spoken to her apart from once when she came over to me last year. I was sharpening a pencil over the bin, and she asked me about my martial arts. I couldn't even talk to her. She must think I'm a mute.

It's happening! Today we were at school and we got issued these really cool camouflage uniforms. We went outside and spent geography and history classes just marching around and learning about the army and discipline and stuff. I didn't see any guns, so I think Jake might have been lying. It was still really exciting though. Phil and I marched together, and during downtime we chatted about the army. Phil said that it was a shame that we'd never need one here. I told him what Jake had said: what would happen if there was a revolt? Phil rolled his eyes in a really obvious I'm-talking-to-an-idiot way and said that there's nothing to revolt for. 'What's the point? Life wouldn't get any better for anyone.' I wondered whether life had ever got better for people after they revolted.

'So why are we doing this at all?' I asked him. I don't know why I asked him. He's my best friend, but he's also sort of an idiot and I don't really care what he thinks.

'I dunno why you're doing it. I'm doing it because I have to. Anyway, it's better than lessons.'

I could have said that that wasn't what I had meant. But there would have been no point. Phil can be really annoying sometimes. I get the impression more and more that he is irritated by me. He only ever wants to talk about ess eee ex these days. It's weird; when we left Earth, he was the same height as me. Now he towers above me.

Still, even though Phil was annoying, it was still an awesome day. It was only at the end of it that I realised I'd barely thought about Hannah at all. Perhaps I should be a soldier. I could be Uncle Jim's personal bodyguard. Although he probably doesn't need one. He could beat up pretty much anyone on the ship.

Dad was very quiet when I told him about my day. Then he closed the door before using the phone. I couldn't hear what he was saying, but his voice was raised the whole time.

The next day, Dad announced at breakfast that he was forming a Citizen's Committee. He said that the cadet training programme was an 'insidious' piece of work by Uncle Jim. I don't know what 'insidious' means, but it sounds like what snakes would say if they could talk. I don't think it's a good thing. This is really bad news though because everyone loves the cadet training at school. If Dad gets it banned then it doesn't matter that Jim is my uncle: I'll be totally ostracised. Social muck. I'm not even sure if Phil would stand by my side.

Dad was on the phone all day while I played computer games in my room. I asked Phil over but he said he was busy, so I just played on my own. Later, the doorbell rang several times, and I could hear people coming in. I recognised one of the voices as Miss Green, who takes us for English. She's about the same age as Dad and has a very soft voice, short brown hair, and slim wrists. Then all I could hear was the rumble of voices. I turned up the volume on the computer and wondered why Phil was busy on the weekend.

In the evening, when everyone had gone and we were eating dinner, I told Dad about Hannah. I don't know why I did, but it felt good to tell someone. I was worried that Dad would dismiss me and want to talk about his lofty ideals, but he didn't. He told me that when he was my age, he'd had a huge crush on this girl in his class. One day he'd finally mustered up the courage to talk to her, and it had turned out that she was quite lonely and welcomed the company. They spent the whole summer together on the beach, making sandcastles and eating ice cream. He told me to ask her round. 'What's the worst that can happen?' were his words. I don't think I can do that. How do you even talk to a girl?

Dad's Citizen's Committee is now an official thing. He's always on the phone, and these days he seems to do everything briskly. He seems happier now he has a purpose. I just hope no one at school finds out. I think they will though, because Miss Green is one of the members. She's always coming round.

When I came in to school today, Phil and Freddie were talking together and laughing. They saw me as I walked in, and stopped talking. Then they looked back at each other and smirked. Phil came over to sit at his desk, in front of mine. I asked him about his weekend, but he didn't really seem in the mood for a long chat.

Our first lesson was with Miss Green. She normally asks me loads of questions (she's onto my making-myself-invisible trick) but today she avoided eye contact. I sat there and looked at Hannah in profile. Once she looked round, and I had to pretend that my glance had merely passed over her on the way to the smartboard. Even as I carried out this charade I felt my cheeks reddening. I didn't dare look at her for the rest of the day. The thought of actually asking her to my house...

Dad asked me this evening if I still thought about Mum a lot. To be honest, Hannah is taking up my whole world at the moment, but I didn't say that. I said that I did but that I wasn't upset any more. He seemed relieved. After supper, he was on the phone again. His voice sounded softer.

My social life is officially over in school after Dad led a peaceful protest on Newton Road outside the Work Sector. Everyone who was going to work ended up seeing Dad and a bunch of other ingrates waving placards saying things like 'A Voice for All' and 'No to Jim's Army!' My one tiny hope was that no one at school would have found out yet. It was brutally crushed. Freddie came up to me, in front of everyone, and I braced myself.

'Your Dad's protesting against Jim, isn't he?' He didn't have to say anything else. I looked down while my hands balled into fists inside my pockets. Freddie sneered at me and walked away. Shame battered me, and I felt like I was hearing everything from inside a vacuum. Faintly, I heard laughter. I looked around for Phil. He was at the back of the crowd, laughing with the rest of them. I just stood there and said nothing.

At lunch, we heard that the protest had been broken up. Miss Jameson came in and told us that Miss Green wouldn't be teaching us today. Freddie, looking at me, asked Miss Jameson if it was true that people had been hurt in the protest. Miss Jameson looked at me and told Freddie that nobody had been seriously hurt. Freddie just sat there with half a smile on his face. I did what I always did: kept my head down and said nothing. I chewed my lip to stop it shaking.

Lunch break was awful. Phil was off with Freddie. They were playing a game where they'd pull the hair of one of the girls or tweak their arm, then run away laughing. The girls squealed but laughed with them. I walked around the playground alone, trying to look as though I had somewhere to go, someone to meet. Lunch break is an hour, but this one crawled by. Science class was even worse. We were meant to pick a partner to do the litmus paper tests with. Normally I'd go with Phil, but today he was with Freddie. I had no partner to go with, so Henry the loser was my partner. I tried to concentrate on the task, but I was aware of all eyes on me. If the rest of my school days are like this then I think I might kill myself.

When I got home, Dad wasn't there. Instead, there was a note out, saying 'Apologies Jason. Your uncle was very heavy handed today, so I'm organising another protest. Must fight the good fight!' Then, underneath, 'Sorry. I know this must be hard.' I'm not sure why I wasn't angrier at Dad. He'd ruined me at school, probably destroyed whatever chance I had with Hannah, but I couldn't quite make myself feel angry at him. I ate my bagmeal alone.

Today was wonderful. The best day of my life. It didn't start that way. I arrived at school and sat down without talking to anyone. Phil totally ignored me. Worse still, Henry said hi. That's an indication that he considers me on his level now. Miss Green wasn't in school again, and I wondered if she was in trouble.

But at break time, it all changed. I was sitting on the fence, alone, pretending to fiddle with my phone, when I looked up and saw Hannah approaching! I looked around, but I was the only person there. She couldn't be coming to talk to anyone else!

'Hey.'

It was definitely me she was talking to. I tried to think of something cool to say, and managed:

'Hey.'

'Can I sit down?'

Of course you can. My God, I'd give all my pocket money for you to sit down next to me.

'Sure.'

She sat down next to me on the fence. Our legs were less than an inch apart. I could smell the product in her hair: fresh, clean. I suddenly worried about how I smelled, and for the first time in my life thought about deodorant. I looked up and tried to control my breathing. She was looking directly at me, and her face couldn't have been more than four inches away from mine. I dropped my eyes; it was like looking at the artificial sun.

'So... I just wanted to say that I thought that the way they treated you yesterday was, like, really mean. My parents think your Dad does good work. Freddie's really nice, I don't think he meant to be mean, but it was all so unfair.'

'Oh. Okay. Thanks. Um. Yeah. Freddie's great, you're probably right. But... thank you.'

'Okay. Well... see you around.'

'Yeah. Err. I mean... see you.'

With that she waltzed off. Fireworks exploded inside my head.

When I got back home, Dad seemed happy too. He was sitting at the dining table with Miss Green. Dad jumped when I came in, and asked me how school was. I gave the usual answer. Miss Green asked me whether I was doing okay given 'what had been going on lately.' I said it was fine. The truth is that I barely noticed them: Hannah's face was in front of my eyes as though burnt onto my retinas.

Today I saw Hannah and Freddie talking. Suddenly, Hannah shouted at him and stormed off. I couldn't hear what they were saying, and of course I said nothing, but inside, I shone like one of the stars outside the windows. Later that day, she came over to me again. This time I found it easier to talk to her, and we chatted for a bit. I felt incredibly grateful to Dad, because it's clear that Hannah supports his actions, and thinks that I do too. In fact, she thinks I'm brave because of it. It made me feel like a bit of a fraud, but not so much that it ruined my happiness.

Hannah told me that her parents would like to invite Dad over. She asked if the two of us wanted to come over Saturday. 'We could just, like, chat and stuff. I think my parents really want to, like, talk to your dad.' I said that I'd ask him.

We walked back into class together, which dramatically increased my rather withered stock of kudos points. I strutted back to my desk, ignoring Phil's disbelieving gaze and Freddie's death stare. The rest of the day went by in a warm fuzzy haze.

Miss Green was home again when I came back. Her and Dad must be really serious about this Citizens Committee thing. I told Dad about Hannah's invitation, and he looked at me for moment. Then he asked whether Hannah was the girl I'd been talking about. I looked at Miss Green, but she laughed and said my secret was safe with her. I nodded.

'In that case,' Dad said, 'I'll definitely accept their invitation.' I could have hugged him, if we'd had that sort of relationship. I thanked him instead, and he and Miss Green shared a happy look.

Today my Dad and I went to Hannah's flat together. All the flats have the same layout, but Hannah's mum had put plants and pictures everywhere. The place felt much more like a home than ours. Hannah's mum had a load of spices and herbs which she used to make the bagmeals seem like a proper dinner. Dad drank wine with Hannah's parents while they all talked about how disgraceful things were and democracy and all that other stuff. I sat at the end of the table with Hannah and relished the opportunity to gaze at her without fear of being caught. We talked about loads of stuff, then Hannah excused herself from the table and asked me if I wanted to come to her room.

My heart pounded as I walked into her room. She'd decorated it with posters of Earth bands, and various girly toys were strewn about the place. She sat down on the bed and motioned to me to join her. I did so next to her, mouth dry.

'Wanna watch something?'

'Sure. Er, whatever you like.' Why did I always sound like such an idiot?

She waved a hand, and the screen came on. She went to the movie menu, and selected something that was just out when we left Earth. Some comedy thing about dinosaurs who travel in time to the present day.

'I'm cold. Let's get under the covers.'

'Oh... okay.'

We both got under the covers, Hannah wriggling in satisfaction. Her knee brushed up against my leg. She didn't move it. I could feel the heat emanating from her body. Her arm came down, her hand casually touching mine. I was afraid to breathe in case I spoiled this perfection.

The movie played on, but I was only conscious of Hannah. Every slight movement was imbued with meaning. Every gesture seemed deliberate. A little way into the movie, she shifted and rested her head on my chest. Her hair was tickly against my chin. I felt as though any happiness that I had had in my life up to now was merely a poor imitation of the real thing. This was real.

Dad came in part way through the movie, smelling faintly of alcohol, to say that we'd better go. He smiled when he saw us curled up under the covers together. As I left, Hannah told me to come round again. I said that I definitely would. I must have said it quite emphatically, because she smiled shyly and looked away.

As we walked back, I sang the theme tune from the movie. After a while, Dad picked it up, and sang along with me.

Cindy George's story 'The Coaster Boys' appeared in our anthology Because of What Happened, *and subsequently won the Writer's Award for that volume. It's nice to have her back again.*

Colouring In
Cindy George

Good at colouring in.

I remember the day at St Sebastian's Primary when we all got our reports, and Max was showing his to everyone because he was so ridiculously pleased about having a 'good at'. I don't think he'd ever had a 'good at' before. Looking back, I think Mr Hinton must have been a bit more creative than some of our other teachers. Think of all the sighing and pen chewing that must have gone on before he finally glanced up at a hamfisted giraffe and realised he'd found something Max was good at.

Mostly, Max was just good at being useless. Everyone liked him a bit because he was nice to people and he was keen to help with things, and he wanted to be friends. But he was slow and awkward and you had to say everything two or three times in different ways before he got it. Any game that included Max always degenerated into a sticky rubble of disaster and confusion, and it was easier to just not let him join in.

The main reason none of us liked him, though, is that he couldn't play football. (That's how you choose your friends when you're eight. My best mate was Jonna Price because he had an Amstrad.) Mr Hinton learned early on that any known method of sorting us into teams invariably ended with Max not crying in a particular way that was obviously very different to a boy with nothing to cry about. So that's how Max became cheerleader, which in Max terms meant running up and down beside the pitch, shouting. He still fell over every now and then, but he usually didn't land in anyone's way.

Mr Hinton's one terrible mistake was not to allow him to do this on the day of our big match against Bilton Juniors.

Presumably thinking Max's cheerleader act might make the pitch look untidy, Mr Hinton had 'promoted' him to what he explained was the terribly important job of the substitute. This involved a certain amount of running on the spot in shorts, but otherwise wasn't too taxing.

That was fine. Max wasn't the sort of kid to get bored. He was the sort of kid who, on school trips to the zoo, never got as far as the aardvarks because he was fascinated by the entry turnstile. He would get left behind on nature walks because he'd stopped to look at a puddle. Max was unboreable.

But on that one day, in that one minute, some spark of wrongness, some germ of restlessness distracted him from his starjumps and stretches, and he started looking around him. Lying on the ground, half hidden behind a fallen branch from a nearby tree, was an intriguing object. Max stared at it for some time.

In the game, Bilton were thrashing us 13–6. We were all down one end of the pitch, terrified of their star striker, a hulking eight-year-old with huge arms and, it was rumoured, his own razor. Mr Hinton was one sugarlump away from swearing.

Nobody was paying any attention to Max, who, responding to the unfamiliar object in the only way that made sense to him, had picked up the biggest stick he could lift, and in a miracle of precision that no one would have expected from him, hit it extremely hard, dead centre.

Almost instantly, he was covered in furious wasps.

Turning towards his screams, we found ourselves for a split second standing motionless before an oncoming squadron of stripy horror. Something stung me on the shin, and I burst into tears and ran to the sidelines, where my dad had his own problems, having been stung right on his bald patch. The Bilton Hulk was stung on the top lip, giving him the pout of a barmaid in a soap opera. Nicholas Taylor found a wasp in his shorts and fainted. Shay Mistry swallowed one. James Woods tried to swat one and got it stuck to his hand; flapping wildly to get it off, he hit little Kev Milligan in the face. Not a single kid went unstung, and through it all there was a terrible buzzing that still sometimes wakes me from bad dreams thirty years later.

When a red and lumpy Mr Hinton carried Max to the ambulance, we assumed he must be dead.

This was a new feeling.

We'd never really thought about Max much, except as a nuisance, but as we stood there, itchy and throbbing, it dawned on each of our unformed brains that one day we too would be dead, and when that happened, one of the things we'd regret would be that we hadn't been nicer to Max. We each surreptitiously decided that if he pulled through, he'd be our best friend.

And we weren't even disappointed when he didn't die. In fact, we were a bit in awe of him for a while, and by the time that wore off he'd grown out of his uselessness, or maybe we'd grown out of being bothered by it.

I still see him for a pint sometimes. He works at the biscuit factory, on the jam rings. He's been there ever since school; they love him there, couldn't manage without him. He reckons it's his dream job.

I got my dream job too, in the end. I doubt I'll ever be as good as my hero, but it feels great to try.

Every September, when I look at my latest intake of fresh, shining pupils, I know that at least one of them is guaranteed to be not much good at anything except colouring in, and I know exactly how valuable that kid is, and how to help them get on.

Cheers for that, Mr Hinton. Cheers, Max.

This brief tale is Die Booth's second story for The Fiction Desk, and a very welcome return. Look for Die's story 'Phantoms' in Crying Just Like Anybody.

Badass
Die Booth

We get all sorts in here. Usually Friday and Saturday nights and weekends, but this one came in on a Tuesday afternoon, face down on a trolley.

He wasn't a teenager, although it was hard to place his age. He had straggly hair the colour of mushrooms and an old Led Zep T-shirt with Superglue spilled down the front, and a thin metal crossbow bolt sticking out of one chunky thigh, just under his left arse-cheek. We were all trying not to laugh. You have to be professional; sympathetic. You get practiced at your game face after a while, but some things are still just funny.

'How'd you manage that?' I asked. *How'd you manage to shoot yourself in your own arse?* He just ground out something about 'it rebounded' through clenched teeth, and that's all he'd say. We had to cut his jeans off really carefully, because the arrow had pushed fabric into the wound. When they came off, he was wearing

Spiderman undies like a little kid. Not actual kid ones – he was too fat, apart from anything else – but those ironic ones they sell in Primark, for blokes who think girls like geeks. You could tell though, him, he was just really into Spiderman. Me and Clive looked at each other over his beached bum and I could see the corners of Clive's mouth twitching and could feel mine doing the same. Just... what possesses some people?

'You'll have a nice scar for the ladies,' I said. He just grunted into his paper pillow. Every time someone touched the arrow he winced, although we'd given him a shot for the pain. When the others went to book him in for surgery and I was left alone with him, I tried to make conversation. I felt kind of sorry for the guy: that stuff that makes a brilliant story in the pub a few years later isn't always such a laugh at the time. 'So, what happened then? Your mate shoot you?'

He gritted his teeth and managed a little headshake. 'No, it was me.'

'So what's the deal? You a re-enactor or something?'

He looked about to cry then, after all that pain. He said,

'I was being Hawkeye.'

I bit my lip. *Must. Not. Laugh.* I felt double sorry for him, although when I retell the story to my mates I never admit that part. I thought of all the stupid crap I've done over the years to impress my mates, to impress girls: jumping over fences and downing yards of ale. Not mucking about with lethal weapons. Maybe he was just more of a badass than me. All these actors in films, they're really lucky I reckon. They're not really superheroes or spies or hard nuts, they're just good looking blokes battering shit out of foam pillars with rubber swords and zipping around on wire harnesses, waiting for the green screen to perform all the heroics. Then when it's all done, they get to see themselves up there, slaying that dragon. I wonder if they ever believe their own hype. And here's us, the rest of us, the audience: stuck with our reality. Sort of makes me think he wasn't that dumb after all. At least he tried.

'Go on,' I said, 'you can tell me. Were you trying to impress a woman?'

He shook his head again, painfully, and he said in this really quiet voice,

'No. It was just for me.'

Dan Purdue's story demonstrates that writing very short fiction successfully means stripping it down to the bear essentials.

The Guy in the Bear Suit
Dan Purdue

The guy in the bear suit does not want to be your friend. He's not here for your amusement. This isn't some accident of whimsy, no accident at all. The guy in the bear suit understands exactly what he's doing. And so do you. You know what this is about.

At first, you hardly noticed him. He was a long way off, the streets were busy, and when you turned, just to rid yourself of that sly prickle bothering the back of your neck, it only took a moment to convince yourself it was nothing more than a fundraising thing or a student prank. Just some bloke in a costume. Nothing to worry about.

That was at the beginning, though. After a while, you began to wonder. How many of those bear suits are out there, anyway? How could it be that you caught sight of one almost every time you left the house? Why the hell would anyone want to dress up as a bear? It seemed it was a sudden craze, and yet nobody at work ever mentioned it.

It didn't take long to learn not to ask anybody else about the guy in the bear suit. Even when he was right across the street, or in that sort-of-courtyard thing outside the office, and you were pointing straight at him. It was always the same, the way they looked at you; that mix of amusement and concern, as though they thought you were telling a joke they didn't quite get. So instead you kept your mouth shut, and you began to worry. You wondered why a guy in a bear suit who seemingly nobody else could see might choose to follow you in particular. You searched for some kind of connection. You… and a guy in a bear suit. Just a bear, even. Nothing came up, but you couldn't shake the feeling that there was something there, right at the back of your mind, just out of reach. You put a lot of effort into finding other things to think about.

The guy in the bear suit. In the distance, almost out of sight but still, undeniably, there. Across the road, standing and watching while you queued for a sandwich. Sitting on a park bench that time you went for a jog to clear your head. Holding onto a trolley at the far end of a supermarket aisle. Sometimes at work the lift doors would open and there he'd be, and you'd have to take the stairs instead. Other times he'd appear outside your kitchen window when you were doing the washing up. One morning he was sitting in your car, right there on the driveway. You had to catch three different buses and you ended up more than an hour late for work. Your colleagues tried to pretend they hadn't been talking about you.

Only now, when you see him in the rain, does it begin to make sense. It's torrential, as though someone is pressure-washing your bedroom window. The guy in the bear suit is outside, standing beneath a streetlight. Just standing there, looking up at the house. You see the water dripping from his paws, running down from his drooping ears. The fur of the suit is three or four shades darker than usual. In the streetlight's glare, the whites of his big eyes glow amber. Now you remember; now you have no choice but to remember: a bear — a normal-sized, toy bear — pulled limp and soggy from the river and held aloft for all to see. You snap the curtains shut before you can think about what they dragged from the water next.

But it's too late. You know why he's here, why he's been getting closer day by day. You know it won't be long before the guy in the bear suit is in the house. It's all you can think about. You imagine how it will play out, picturing yourself looking up into the grinning mouth, the blank stare of those big plastic eyes. The feel of that cold, wet fur on your skin. You practise your objections, your pleas. Your lips move as you imagine yourself trying to explain how you'd only ever meant to scare him, how you'd only been a kid, the same as he was. No one could have predicted what happened. You'd had no idea how strong the current was there, or how cold the water. You know it won't make any difference. You can't even convince yourself.

When you summon the courage to look outside again, the guy in the bear suit is gone from under the streetlight. You run from room to room, squinting out into the darkness, carrying like a torch in front of you the absurd hope you'll see him walking away. You don't, of course. He's not going to give up now, not when he's waited so long.

The doorbell rings. You stand in the hall, motionless, your joints locked with fear. Rain lashes the windows. The guy in the bear suit does not want to be your friend. You know what this is about.

We publish many wonderful stories from creative writing graduates around the world, but sometimes there's no substitute for lived experience. Alex Clark's background as an industrial archaeologist brings this supernatural tale to life.

The Stamp Works
Alex Clark

Do you go to church?

I do. Every Sunday, for the last five years. Ever since the Stamp Works.

Doesn't matter which kind; last week it was the Catholics, next week maybe the Baptist chapel. I know all the times and the routines now, so I can pitch it minute-perfect. I come in late, sit at the back, leave before the last song's finished. Avoid the minister, put a decent bit of change in the collection plate, and I've done my duty for another week.

I wasn't raised that way. Wasn't even baptised. My dad's a good, solid, hard-headed man, no time for politics or God. My mum's people were Catholic, but she hasn't been to church since she was fifteen, and after she married my dad the family didn't speak to her much. So we were raised on love and logic, and that's a great combination, but it left a few big things out. Things I wasn't prepared for. And that's why you'll find me on my knees once a week: I've got a big debt to pay off, and I'm paying it in the only way I can think of.

Don't worry, I won't try to convert you. A man can only speak for himself, and it's none of my business what you believe, or whether you believe me. I'm not even sure what I believe myself. But I can tell you what happened, and you can make some sense of it for yourself.

I used to be an archaeologist. Not the digging kind, or the television kind: an industrial archaeologist. I work at the archives now — easier on my nerves — but back then I had a little company, High Peak Archaeology. That's a grand name, but what it meant was me and Nicky, a kid I'd taken on from university. Only two of us, but that's all we needed. When Sheffield got back on the up again, round the start of this century, all those rotten old steelworks and factories were suddenly prime estate. Trouble was, once the developers bought one they soon found out that they had to pay someone to come round and record the place as it was, those great wrecks being part of Our Industrial Heritage. It was us, at a good price per day, or no planning permission. We spent our days tramping round derelict workshops, photographing their last dying days before reincarnation as an Exciting Mixed-Use Development. We forced open their rusted gates and shone torches into boarded, long-dark offices; we drew their rambling floorplans and sliced sections through their sagging floors as though we were conducting an autopsy. And when we had finished we handed in our report and consigned the buildings to the grave.

The Stamp Works was a big contract. I was surprised when our tender was accepted, but it turned out the developers, Orson Bright Ltd, needed the job doing before the end of November and we were the only ones who could move quickly enough. They were insistent: we had to start work straight away, in the third week in October. It wasn't ideal. The nights were drawing in and we were forecast another two weeks straight of rain, on top of the one we'd already had, and with the cloud lying so heavy over the city it was half dark by the afternoon. Most of these old places had no power, some no roof; what windows there were were often boarded.

Then again, it was nothing we hadn't done before. We were gung-ho, proud of our resilience. We had worked through last December in an abandoned factory, sheltering the clipboards with our five-layer-muffled bodies as the snow drifted down through the roof and settled over the junkie leavings. We had drawn until our fingers got too stiff to bend, and we had got the job in on time, with a tidy profit. We had seen it all. The needles, the rats, the graffiti, the rooms covered ceiling to floor in perfect yellow mushrooms feasting on the wallpaper's animal glue. We were the first in, before the health and safety men, before the floors were stabilised and the pigeons cleared out, before the asbestos was found and the addicts evicted. We were afraid of nothing.

And on top of that, if I'm honest, I needed the money. Christy had moved out six months previous, to her sister's, and there was only one way that was going to end. Half of what I had wasn't enough to live on, for a man of forty-five. Not nearly enough. And maybe that's why I did what I did. Desperation makes a lot of bad decisions.

It was five to eight on a Thursday morning when we first pulled up outside the Stamp Works, down a neglected little road low in the Don Valley. We had turned off the main road a mile or so back, passing a few rows of seedy-looking terraces and a closed pub, then a scrubby wasteland of concrete bases and skeletal steel frames. Beyond this, as we approached the foggy edge of the river, the rotting carcases of smaller warehouses and sheds emerged, getting gradually larger and more substantial until we reached, abruptly, two massive steel-barred gates in a tall black-brick wall. They marked the end of the road, and to their right, half-hanging from the wall, was a metal sign with the words Stamp Works: Joshua Stamp, Cutlers. Through the gloom and the never-ending screen of water, we couldn't see much of the main buildings; just a large black shape outlined against the grey sky.

'Beautiful,' said Nicky. We sat for a while in silence looking at the gates and the rain.

'He said eight o'clock, yeah?'

'Yes,' I said.

'Are you sure he's not meeting us inside?'

I wasn't. It had got to five past eight, so I pulled the hood of my waterproof up and opened the door of the van.

The gates were secured with an iron chain and a massive padlock. Unless the bloke had locked us out, he was meeting us this side. As I turned to go back to the van, though, I noticed a modern intercom box attached to bricks on the left-hand gatepost.

With the water now beginning to stream off my waterproof onto my thighs, I stepped over to it. It looked recent. There was a speaker grille and an unlabelled grey button next to it. I pressed it. I expected the buzz of an intercom, but there was nothing. I kept my finger on the button and leant my face into the grille. 'Hello?' I shouted. 'Hello? This is Andy, here to meet John. John Straker. Hello?'

There was nothing. I let the intercom button go. It had obviously been disconnected, or no one was there. The manager was just late. And, as if by magic, at that moment I heard the distant noise of an engine coming down the road behind us.

I turned to see the approaching car. I was straining my eyes through the rain, and my ears to hear the engine. People have told me since that it was the sound of the water on my hood, or the hum of the vehicle, or the sound of rubbish crumpling under my footsteps. But I know better. It was a crackle, a sharp electric cry, and it came from the intercom.

I didn't think much of it at the time. I half turned, but there was the car, a smart red Audi; in a moment it had pulled up beside us, and John Straker stepped out.

He didn't look much like a site manager. He was tall and well groomed, with a narrow build and neat greying hair. He was wearing a suit beneath his perfectly clean high-visibility waterproof, and his shoes were shiny black. He swung his feet sideways as he put them down on the road, to avoid a patch of mud.

'Hi. Andy, I presume?'

I said yes, I was, and he introduced himself as John, so unlikely or not, we had our manager. I called Nicky out and introduced him, and John pulled a few sheets of paper and an enormous bunch of keys from his car.

'This is all we've got, I'm afraid,' he said, handing the papers to me. 'The factory — it was a cutlery works, you know that already? Good. It closed fifteen years ago, and no one's done anything with it since. Some kids broke in a while ago and started a fire in the offices, so we've lost most of the records, plans, all that stuff.'

'Okay, no problem,' I said. 'We'll do our search at the county archives anyway. Maybe they've got something. What's the condition of the buildings?'

He looked embarrassed. 'Ah. I don't know much, I'm afraid. I've only been involved since the purchase.'

It turned out he worked for the developers. There had been no caretaker on the site since it closed.

Apart, I said, from the security guard.

He was looking through the bunch of keys, and he took a moment to answer me. Looking back now, I must have given him a nasty shock with that question. But he covered it well. No, he said, there was no security guard now. He had been laid off when the developers bought the buildings. We would be alone on site.

He picked out a key from the collection and opened the padlock, pushing the gates in to allow space for the van to fit through. I had been expecting rust, but they swung round smoothly and without noise. Then he stepped back and held the keys out to me.

'Are you not giving us an induction?' I said.

He looked awkward. 'No steelies,' he said, poking one foot out at me. 'Can't go beyond the gate, I'm afraid. Anyway, you know as much as I do. Sorry I can't be more help.'

This kind of thing isn't supposed to happen, but as I said, we were gung-ho. They were supposed to show us round, tell us where the holes in the floor were, how to get in and out of the buildings. But we needed the money — I needed the money — and beggars can't be choosers. And we were indestructible. We'd seen it all before.

'Okay,' I said.

As he turned and tracked his way back round the puddles to his car, I had a thought. 'You're all right for us to use the power?' I called.

Through the grey veil, I saw him turn his head and yell, 'There isn't any power. It's been turned off.'

'But the intercom,' I called. 'It works.'

I don't know whether he heard me, but as he ducked his head into his car he yelled again, 'The electric was disconnected weeks ago. Sorry.' And he was gone.

The Stamp Works

The main yard of the Stamp Works was a dismal place. It was cobbled, a remnant of the Victorian era. Around it on three sides, in a U shape, rose tall brick-built workshops populated by hundreds of iron-framed windows, the unboarded frames sporting ragged fangs of shattered glass. The west range, one arm of the U, was to our left, and the central range stood ahead of us. To our right was the east range, only two storeys high. Black fire scars flared up from its windows, which had been blocked with plywood, now sodden and warped. Bushes grew from the sills, and pigeons drooped, dejected, on the pieces of broken ironwork that projected from the walls.

Beyond the central yard was a complex of dilapidated warehouses and vehicle sheds, sinking slowly into the ground, all of them scrawled with spray paint and strewn with cans and bottles. The great black engineering-brick wall, which surrounded it all like a fortress, ended by the river in a chain-link fence into which a gaping hole had been hacked. We had seen worse, but it was a miracle the whole site hadn't already been burnt to the ground.

'Jesus,' said Nicky, standing in the middle of the yard and looking up at the sway-backed roofs. 'What a dump.'

'Get the torches out,' I said, 'and we'll see what we're looking at.'

One set of doors to the yard workshops, at the near end of the west range, hadn't been boarded but were fitted with big steel gates, opened by one of the many keys in John Straker's bunch. All of the other doorways were blocked, covered in heavy ply and nailed over with batons. To get to the east range we would need to walk round through the west and central ranges.

We wedged the doors firmly open and made our way into the still, dim interior.

It could have been worse, we agreed. It was dry. The floors were intact. The windows gave a grey light that meant we could see without our torches, if necessary. We made our way past the dust-heavy workbenches, along the rows of iron columns that marched across the long narrow rooms. Nicky began to cheer up. He loved the mystery of exploring somewhere abandoned. I waited for him a few times while he rooted around on the floor in the dirt, returning with a bent apostle spoon or a little wooden presentation box.

We tracked across the ground floor and up wide stone steps, dished with a hundred years of footfall, to the first, second, third floors. There were pigeons at the top, the rooms covered in thick, sour-smelling guano and the awkward mummified remains of birds, but we had masks in the van and we'd dealt with that problem before.

Everything was looking fine until we found ourselves at the entrance to the east range.

We saw the doorway first at a distance, at the end of yet another long, empty, dusty workshop. It looked like the far wall was covered with a great, grey flower. For a minute I thought it was some more graffiti, until we got close enough to make out the perfectly black rectangle at its centre, and smell the breath, even all this time after the event, of charred wood, soot, and smoke.

We had turned our torches off a while ago, conserving the batteries while we had natural light, but now we both switched them on again and swung the beams into the opening. Beyond it was a stairwell, rising to the first floor, and at its base a door into the ground-floor rooms. This had been fitted with a new steel shutter, padlocked shut. It took us fifteen minutes to find out that none of the keys John Straker had given us fitted it.

'He'll have to come back and sort it out,' I said to Nicky. 'Someone's got the keys. It's only just been fitted.'

He pointed his light up the stairway. 'Shall we?'

We followed it up, our boots kicking up puffs of powdery soot. We were safe enough on the stairs, I knew, because they were stone. Beyond that, we'd see what it was like up there. Burnt buildings are unpredictable. You don't know where the damage is. A floor may look safe, but you walk across the wrong place and you're a cautionary tale. If you have to do it, stick to the walls and hope the ends of the joists are secure. I'd told Nicky that before, but I told him again as we climbed up that acrid staircase into the gloom; he needed telling everything twice. He was a skater, a BMX kid, coming to work every Monday with a new hard-earned array of scrapes and bruises to show me. He was at that age when he was still immortal, not much past his twenty-first birthday.

I needn't have worried. We couldn't get the door open. It was a modern office door, orange, soot-stained but not much damaged by the fire, and someone had fixed a bolt to the outside and secured it with a shiny new padlock. I think we both knew, before we tried the keys, that none of them would fit.

Heading back through the west range, Nicky disappeared again, darting off into one of the side rooms near the doors. I don't know what he noticed; maybe a trail in the dust, maybe the new wiring, but we'd missed it on the first walk-through: a clean little room, panelled out in painted ply, with a new half-glass door, housing a little table, a couple of chairs, some plug points and a kettle. A chipped floral mug sat on the side, perfectly clean and upturned as if it had been washed and left to dry.

'It's the old security guard's room,' said Nicky. He was fiddling with a little grey box on the wall, the other end of the intercom system. 'Could be a good base. Awesome, a kettle!'

It didn't take much to please us. A clean indoor room was a bonus, and a kettle was luxury. I disappointed him by flicking the switch on and off. 'No power,' I said. 'Disconnected weeks ago.'

He took this well. 'It's still a good room. We can leave all the stuff here. If it's raining we can have our lunch breaks here. I'm going to bring the gear in.'

After he left, I walked over to the intercom and pressed the button. I don't know what I was expecting, but nothing is what I got.

The first week went easy enough. We got the lights set up, running them off the generator which we set up in the courtyard, underneath a makeshift tarpaulin roof to keep off the never-ending rain. We fed cables from it through the west range doors so that we could light up the shadowy floors with merciless, all-conquering halogen glare, and when we needed to move into the central range, we threaded them through broken windows and round loose bits of ply, like long wiry roots curling around the dead bulk of the brickwork. We completed the photographic record, the painstaking work of three whole days with camera, lights, and register, every picture numbered and located for posterity. The plans were well under way, skeleton outlines filling in slowly with walls, doors, windows, beams, workbenches, machinery. There were only two problems: the east range and the soot.

Of the two, the east range access problem was the clearer. John Straker had stopped answering his calls. He'd answered the first time, hedged the question of the keys for the two locked doors, and then simply disappeared off the radar.

'Bastard,' I said to Nicky, after the fifth unanswered call. 'He just can't be bothered to sort it out.'

'Tell him he won't get consent unless the record's complete,' said Nicky.

I had, but even that didn't seem to inspire him. 'Sod him,' I said. 'We'll give him half a record, and he'll be back on the phone in a month saying he needs the rest.'

The soot was a far stranger problem.

At first we thought, each of us, that we must have trodden on our drawing boards. You lodge a board anywhere you can while you're drawing, and when you need to take a measurement sometimes the floor's the only place to put it. A bootprint on a drawing isn't unusual, but it doesn't matter too much. They get traced into a nice clean version on the computer later. So I didn't think much about it when I put my board on the floor, measured a window, turned back to it and found a little black splodge on the edge of my plan. Neither, I found out later, did Nicky, at the same moment on the floor above me. A puff of breath and it was gone.

The next time I put the board down, it came back.

It was bigger this time, an odd, pitch-black Rorschach shape on the pale drawing. It was well defined, raised, dense, and fine; not a print or a stain, but a deposit. When I angled the board it slid off, leaving behind a grey ghost of itself.

The third time I put the board down, as the day was beginning to draw in and the shadows behind the halogen halo became darker and more defined, I half expected it. I didn't pick it up for a moment, but stood gazing at it. You'll think I'm daft, but I had to have a very firm word with myself before I reached out for that drawing, mainly concerning common sense and Occam's razor. In the end I snatched at it and knocked it against the wall in one movement, pretending I didn't see the silent runnel of soft black particles that drifted down towards the desiccated floor.

Nicky was waiting for me in the office – now our office – when I got back. I'd packed it in ten minutes early, unnerved and angry at myself for it, so I was surprised to see him standing next to the sink scrubbing at his drawing with a paper towel.

He tried to deny it when I asked him, but I showed him my grey-coated drawing board and told him to leave off.

He looked at me for a moment, then said simply, 'It's soot.'

'It must be dropping from the ceiling,' I said, though I didn't sound like I'd even convinced myself.

'Where is it?' Nicky said.

'What?'

'On your board. Which bit.'

I looked at the drawing. The little molecules of soot were still clinging there, the lines of my plan visible behind them. The area they inhabited had not been filled in with detail: it was a blank outline box, with the words NO ACCESS printed on it in pencil.

'It's the east range,' I said.

'Mine too,' he said, and turned back to his scrubbing with greater violence.

We packed up in silence. As we drove out through the gates, almost as if he had waited to be out of earshot of the works, Nicky said, 'Did you notice what it looked like?'

I shook my head as I stopped the car and put my hood up.

'It looked like someone falling,' he said distantly.

I got out of the car, into the deluge, and pushed the great steel gates shut on another day.

We never talked about the soot again, or mentioned the things we did to protect against it, though we both knew what was going on. Nicky made holes in two corners of his board with his dad's drill and tied a cord between them, so he could hang it round his neck or carry it under his arm like a bag, and never had to leave it out of sight. Me, I folded the drawing in two so that the east range was turned back on itself, hidden. It worked.

On the Wednesday of the next week, the archive material arrived at my house, a neat little brown-paper package containing copies of all the documentary evidence in the local archives relating to the Stamp Works. Ordinarily we'd go to the county library and do the search ourselves, but with the rush on this job I'd chosen the easier but more expensive option of getting the archivist to do it and send us everything relevant.

After tea, I sat down at the table and looked through it. It was a muddle of the usual stuff: yellowing group photos of workers from the twenties, the men granite faced and uncompromising, the women nervous and stiff; sixties blueprints of new plumbing schemes; Victorian adverts announcing that 'A Large Variety of Tableware is Held in Stock.' I picked out the useful stuff: scale plans, photos of the buildings, maps. There was enough there to tell me that the east range had been the engine room, the heart of the factory, housing a massive beam engine driven by steam. This monster had run the rattling networks of axles that turned the belts on the machines; if there was any of it left, it was one of the most important parts of the building. And also the one part we couldn't get into.

I flicked through the more modern material as I listened, for the twentieth time, to John Straker's answerphone greeting. We hadn't put an upper time limit on the search, so we had a few modern newspaper articles: the fire was there ('Arson Blaze at Don Valley Factory'), and a snippet about the site purchase ('Developers Orson Bright confirm exciting new plans for Stamp Works site'), and then, last of all, something dated only a couple of weeks ago. I was hanging up on Straker when the words 'severe injuries' caught my attention.

'Jason Woods, 25, of Tinsley, is in a critical state at the Northern General Hospital following an incident at the Don Valley Stamp Works site. Mr Woods, a security guard at the derelict site, suffered an accident on Monday night and was taken to hospital with severe head injuries. He remains in a coma. The nature of the accident is unclear, but is being investigated by representatives of developers Orson Bright, owners of the works.'

He hadn't called in as usual on Tuesday morning, so the security company had sent someone out to check on him. They found him a few feet from his office, lying on the floor, with a fractured skull. There was nothing to say how it happened.

I looked at the photocopy for a little while, and thought about John Straker. Nothing too complimentary, I can tell you. I thought about ringing him and telling him to stuff the job. I thought about ringing the police and telling them we'd been sent into a dangerous site, maybe even a deadly site, without warning or protection. I thought about Nicky, and how young he was, how keen, and how easily damaged.

In the end I rang the hospital. They were reluctant to tell me anything, but the nurse sounded harassed and I told her I was Jason's uncle. I'm not proud of it, but it worked. He was still there, and he hadn't woken up. Whatever he knew, he couldn't tell me yet.

I sat and thought for a long time, looking at that photograph of a lad with a stupid trendy haircut and a big open grin, lying now on a sterile white bed with the beeps of the monitors for company.

They must have known that we wouldn't do the job if they told us about the accident. That would put even me off. They didn't know what had happened, or where it had happened, or whether it would happen again. We'd been in those buildings for a week and a half, and they were buildings that might contain a deathtrap. They had concealed this from us, to get the job done quickly, to keep their development moving on.

Then again, there was the money. It was a good rate Orson Bright were paying us — very good — the kind of money you pay when you need a job doing fast, with no complications. And I needed it. The way I saw it, it was my choice. I could carry on, if I was careful. I was a veteran. I could do the rest of the work — we were almost there, anyway — and collect my cash prize.

But I couldn't ask Nicky to go back there. I would have to do it alone. Lone working was a bad idea, but not as bad as taking an over-confident kid into a lethal site.

I decided to ring him in the morning, but in the event I didn't have to. When I turned on my phone there was an answerphone message from him, left at 5am, saying he was really sorry but he was calling in sick. He sounded exhausted. If I hadn't been so relieved about getting out of an awkward conversation, I'd have been worried about him; but I was just happy for the coincidence. Christy always did say I couldn't see beyond the end of my own nose, and as I tell you this I can't help wondering if she was right. I should have asked him what was wrong with him: it was one of the warning signs. But I didn't. And that's why this story ends the way it does.

I finished the plans. It didn't take long: a couple of days. Nicky's work was good, clear, and it wasn't difficult to pick up where he left off. I ate my packed lunches alone, in Jason Woods' bare little office, and I stopped taking tea breaks. I wanted to get out of there, I'll admit it. I wanted to pack up and never see the place again, and the faster I worked, the nearer that day came. Except that, at the end of it all, after all the photos and the drawing and the notes, I was left with a big blank space in my lovely detailed record.

The east range. The most important bit of the site. The only bit I couldn't get into.

I don't think I intended to break in. It had just been one of those days: the cables knotting themselves like landed eels, snagging and disconnecting themselves; the bloody sodding rain still going, an endless, thrumming, sound-flattening din; the generator stalling and refusing to start again, me pulling the cord until I was sweaty and pissed off, and still nothing; and then suddenly, there I was, at the top of the stairs, looking at that orange office door. Everything was going wrong; the shitty weather, that bastard Straker, and being alone, and Christy, and now the building itself was taunting me, stopping me moving on, keeping me there in that endless grey Purgatory.

It wasn't the padlock that gave, but the screws that fixed the hasp to the door. They were only fixed in a few mil of board, and they wrenched out with just one good kick. I stood there, panting, hearing the bang echo away to nothing, and the darkness on the other side looked at me.

I looked back at it, and then I went and got my board.

I would have to work by headlamp. The cables from the generator wouldn't reach up the stairs, and I was in no mood to try threading them through the boarded-up openings. I was so full of anger and adrenaline that I didn't care. I wouldn't own to it, but I can see now that I couldn't stand to feel afraid. I had snapped, and when you snap you throw everything out, the good sense with the bad, and you do things like walking alone into an unknown, fire-damaged building with only a headlamp to guide you. Remember that. Fear does strange things to a person, and if you ever find yourself in the same way, just think of me and maybe it'll save you a whole lot of grief.

The lamp shone a beam of brightness ahead of me, but left the shadows to either side untouched. The first thing I saw when I looked through the door was a desk; then another, then another. I stayed in the doorway, and played the beam over the room as far as it would go, which wasn't very far at all.

It must have been their sales office, maybe sometime in the nineties, just before the place closed down. It was a long room, receding into the black ahead of me, and down the wall on each side ran ranks of desks, still bearing in-trays, sheaves of paper, folders, pen-holders. The computer monitors had gone, but the phones remained: old-fashioned, clunky plastic jobs, one at the corner of each desk. The chairs were there, all in different positions and at different angles, as if the staff had just pushed them back, got up and walked out. And everything, absolutely everything, was covered in a thick, silent coating of pitch-black soot.

The actual fire damage wasn't too bad, at least at this end of the room, and I wondered where it had been started; perhaps at the other end of the range. Fires can carry soot a long way, and a place looks bad, but underneath it's pretty sound. I said this to myself as I took my first steps in, shining the light at the floor, seeing ruined carpet beneath my feet.

It was impossible to stick to the walls. The desks were in the way. I walked, slowly, down the middle of the room, moving the light here and there as I went, making tiny bright tableaux in the void. A bookshelf, a fire exit sign, an extension cable. A poster, smoke-damaged and unreadable, hanging from the wall. I tested the floor beneath my feet with every step, waiting for the bounce that meant the joists were hanging free, but it felt solid.

The brick walls had been clad out in board. Any clues to where the old engine room had been were disguised beneath the modern fittings. Progressing, leaving the doorway and its square of grey light further and further behind me, I swung the light up into the roof, looking for any evidence of a chimney. I was expecting a boarded office ceiling, but astonishingly it was open to the rafters, a massive, beautiful king-post timber roof, original

Victorian work, and I really should have stopped moving forwards as I raised my head and stared at it, but I didn't. I carried on walking, carried on putting my feet down onto the unknown, and I'd taken six steps precisely when it happened.

For a second it was like the world exploding. I couldn't tell what it was but it was everywhere, it was everywhere, it filled my head and stopped me dead where I stood, and then I realised I had my hands over my ears and the reason was the telephones. They were ringing. All of them, on every desk, in unison; a heart-stopping screaming wall of noise. And — you must believe me now — when I say in unison, I mean in unison. All of them, maybe thirty phones, perfectly synchronised, each ring, each pause, each ring. Immaculate. Impossible. And like a madman, because it was enough to make me one, I can tell you, I reached down to the nearest one and picked it up.

And they stopped.

And when I looked down at the handset in my grip — because something in me stopped me putting it to my ear, and I'll always wonder what I would have heard if I had — and saw the burned cable end hanging from the mouthpiece, connected to nothing, I threw it away from me like it was something dead.

It took me a while, standing there frozen to the spot, in that dreadful black void, before I realised it had taken an awfully long time to hit the floor.

I dropped my head, and the lamp with it, and I knew what I'd see before it showed me.

My toes were within a foot of the drop. Beyond that, there was nothing; the whole middle section of the floor gone, burned out by the inferno that had started on the ground floor. It was a great coal-black pit, and the light from the lamp got lost in it, but as my eyes adjusted I could just make out the surface of the concrete below, a long way below; and on it, lying where they had fallen, in a halo of smashed glass, the telephone handset and a security guard's torch.

They paid me, in the end. I sent what I had to John Straker, and I accompanied it with a photocopy of the article about poor Jason Woods, and though we never spoke about it, a nice, prompt transaction deposited my full fee into my bank account three days later. It must have been a few days after that that the police went calling on him; or at least I hope they did. They sounded interested enough when I spoke to them. I don't know what happened to Orson Bright; the Stamp Works is still there, at any rate. The top two floors of the west range were gutted by fire last Christmas, and English Heritage have started getting shirty about it being left to fall to bits, so probably it'll have another bright new future very soon.

I saw Nicky in a pub not long after I sent the stuff to Straker. He said he was better and ready to come back to work, but I wanted to know what had happened to him. I had my suspicions.

'You'll think I'm daft,' he said. He didn't look old enough to be drinking the pint he was holding. He was slight, discomfited, huddled in his oversize T-shirt.

'Try me,' I said.

'I kept having these dreams,' he said, looking at the table. 'Weird ones. About the Stamp Works.'

He was waiting to be ridiculed, I could tell, so I said, 'Me too,' though I hadn't. He looked up at me, hopefully.

'Really?'

'Yeah. Tell me what yours were about first.'

He traced a line on the table with his finger, unwilling even at this distance to relive the nightmares. 'It was always the same,' he said. 'Sometimes four or five times a night. It just kept replaying.

In the dream I'm standing in the works — I think it's the central range but I can't tell really, it looks like everywhere else in there, just a big long room with columns going across it — and I'm at one end of the room, and I'm looking at the other.' He paused, and took a drink.

'The other end of the room is dark, very dark, and I can't see what's there but I'm trying. I'm straining my eyes in the dark, because I know there's something there. I don't know how, but I know.' He looked up at me for reassurance, and I nodded to show I was with him.

'And as I stare, and wait, and stare, I start to think I can see something. Something kind of low to the ground, like a big animal on all fours, and it's moving slowly but it's moving towards me, coming out of the shadows, and as I watch it come closer I can see that it's a man.'

I nodded again but I'd gone cold and clenched inside. I knew what he was going to say.

'In the dream I can't move,' he said. 'So I have to wait there, and watch this man. He's crawling, and I can tell it's really hard for him. It's like he's hurt. He's dragging himself forward, and he's desperate, I don't know what for. Sometimes he stops and lies down on the floor, and I think he's dead, but then he pulls himself up again and he keeps going, and I wish he was dead, because —' Nicky took a deep breath, and I put my hand on his shoulder. Even in broad daylight in a Sheffield pub parlour I could see that long dusty room, and that jerky, dying form pulling itself out of the shadows.

'I can't move,' he said, 'and by the end he's close enough to me to touch, and he stops, and he's right in front of me, and his head's hanging down, and then he raises it up and he looks at me.' He raised his own head and looked me in the eye. 'And I see his face,' he said.

'Drink the rest of that,' I said, and I got up and went to the bar and bought him whisky. Yeah, I know it doesn't help, but it was the only thing I could think of to do. I could imagine what he'd seen. I could imagine what a twelve-foot drop onto a concrete floor did to a man's appearance.

I told him to see his friends more. Go biking, I said. The dreams have stopped, there's nothing wrong with you, so don't worry. Get out into the open and the fresh air. Some day this will all seem a long time ago.

He's bounced back remarkably well. It must be youth. He's working with a friend of mine, and he shows no sign of being troubled, other than an aversion to the smell of soot. He's got a girlfriend now, Anya, and she fills his head with the future. He'll be okay.

I tried to see Jason. It was a good week later, because I couldn't pluck up the courage to do it earlier, but eventually I rang the hospital again and they were sorry to inform me that Mr Woods had passed away. If I wanted to express my condolences I could donate to charity on the webpage his family had set up.

I did, and I also found out where he was buried, which led me to be standing on a freezing east Sheffield hilltop on a windy November morning, holding a bunch of flowers. He had a small headstone, which was swamped in blooms, just on the turn. I laid mine with the rest, near the foot end so they didn't stand out. I had wanted to talk to him, but as I stood there and stared at the black granite I didn't know how. After a minute I knelt down close to the ground, self-consciously, and said quietly, 'I know, Jason.' I paused, while the wind whipped across my face. 'They didn't check the buildings properly. And you knew they'd do the same to someone else. And they did, because when their investigators found out what happened they didn't say anything, they just locked up the rooms and sent us in.' I was crying by then, but the weather carried it off, and I didn't feel the tears on my face.

'The papers said you went at 4:22pm on Monday. I reckon that was the same time you rang me.' I stopped, and thought of the screaming of the monitors in one part of the city, and of a room of shrilling, disconnected phones in another.

'Thank you,' I said.

And then I left.

So, what's all this got to do with God, you'll say? You started by talking about church, and your debt to pay, and what's that got to do with it?

Well, the way I see it, it's about power. Jason didn't have the power to do what he needed to do, what he was desperate to do: to protect us. Not while he was here, in the world. He was in flux, a weak charge, his signal kept failing. But when he was leaving, in that moment between heaven and earth... ah, in that moment he was a lightning bolt, a direct current, a charge to blow fuses and raise monsters, an arc light that left no shadow. In that moment he was a force of God, and in that tiny moment he reached out and saved my life.

So that's why I pray. It's the least I can do. That and tell people, because you never know when a cautionary tale may do some good.

And now, if you'll excuse me, I have an appointment at the cathedral. It's Sunday morning, and the service starts at eleven.

We're seeing more short stories from Australia and New Zealand these days. Melissa Goode is based just outside Sydney.

Exile
Melissa Goode

With his legs crossed, he smoothes a hand down the sharp angle of his leg and it rests on his knee. The ends of his fingers, under the nails, are white. It is the only indication of what he is thinking. I had not forgotten that his legs were endless. Those hands are just the same: long fingers and each bone articulated. He does not look at me, but at the whisky in his glass.

He is wearing a black suit and black shoes. I was kind, giving him notice: an hour's notice. I would have liked to catch him out, wearing a T-shirt and boxers and hugging his cat. He never did keep regular hours. But he is wearing his suit, with his dark hair wet from the shower and a crisp white shirt stark against his jacket. I could have caught him out.

I stood on his front step for maybe ten minutes before I rang the doorbell. It was freezing. The sky dark and snow swirling under the fluorescent white street lamps. I certainly remember that snow.

The terrace houses opposite have windows of gold light. This is London, the privileged end of London. His terrace house is still painted white and the door is still painted the same bright blood red.

I was relieved that he opened the door to me. He watched me for a moment as if weighing or calculating something. Then he kissed both of my cheeks slowly, European style. It was as if he knew that one day I would again appear on his doorstep, and today happened to be that day. Against his warm lips, my cheeks were cold, as if I were dead. He did not say 'Hello'; instead he said, 'You are so cold,' and I was relieved that he had not lost his Australian accent.

Upstairs, a door slams and it is sharp and singular, like a gunshot.

'Who was that?' I ask.

Fast footsteps thud down the wooden staircase, followed by a few swishing steps across the tiled floor of the entryway, and the front door slams so hard that I feel it in my ribs.

He looks up at me, as if having forgotten that I was there. 'Henry. My son. You remember him?'

Of course I remember him, although my memory is outdated by ten years. I remember a six-year-old boy watching me over his large book, his thin legs stuck out in front of him on the lounge. The book hid his mouth, but from his stare I imagined the curl of his lip.

'He must be all grown up now,' I say.

'He is. Sixteen.' He smiles. 'But he is angry. I remember being that thoughtless and awful and angry when I was his age. I have to remember that. Every fucking day I have to remember that.'

It is the most he has said to me since I arrived.

'I suppose teenagers have a lot to be angry about,' I say.

'Well, he certainly does,' he says, but does not explain, keeping that story to himself. He drains his glass.

On the coffee table between us is a Bible. For a moment, I struggle to drag my eyes away from it. The Bible is a surprise, although it shouldn't be. He was always looking for something. *So, the Buddhism didn't work?* I could say, but I won't. I should be grateful that he even let me back into his house.

He inhales sharply as he stands. A silver crucifix around his neck glints, swinging, as he gets out of his seat.

'Another drink?' he says at the same time as I say, 'And Isabel?'

He stands there, the glass hanging from his hand, watching me. He could ignore my question and pretend he did not hear it. I would even play along with his pretence, because what a thing for me to ask.

'She left a good five years ago,' he says, quietly, and bends to take my empty glass from the coffee table.

'Another?' he asks, already walking towards the drinks cabinet.

'Yes, please.'

I get out of the armchair and walk to the tall window. It lets in the dim London winter afternoon and it may as well be night.

It is quiet. It is so quiet here that I hear the glug of whisky into the glasses. I fancy that I hear him swallow, but it is only my imagination; he is too far away. With his head bent, he walks with the two glasses towards me. His steps are sharp against the wooden floor and muted when he crosses onto the silk Persian rug. He is probably wondering when I am going to leave: leave him to get back to his Bible.

He is older now — ten years older — but then so am I. He hands me the glass and I feel his fingers as I take it from him. I can smell his shaving cream. By the window, away from the lamp's circle of yellow light and away from the glow of the fireplace, the light is gloomy, grey-blue. He looks down at me. This face used to smile for me. I did not have to do anything and it smiled.

Perhaps he is seeing what I am seeing in him: lines in the forehead, around the mouth and at the corners of eyes. But whatever is in my face, it is stronger in his. He will always be seventeen years older than me and now the aging is accelerating, gathering pace. His fiftieth birthday would have been last week.

The cold comes through the window. I touch my fingers to the frozen glass.

'You look just the same,' he says.

I look up at him. There is a twist of his mouth, as if more words were coming. But whatever he was going to say, he does not say it.

'Despite everything?' I say.

'What is everything?'

'Well, ten years of the Australian climate. It can be hard on a woman's complexion.'

His gaze lengthens. Is he remembering the burning blue skies of his childhood in Melbourne? Is he remembering that he was going to come back home with me to Australia? Although I now see that for the fantasy it was. He would never leave his son. I should have known that. The heavy unconditional love for a child outweighed whatever we had.

'I don't think I could look the same,' I say. 'I was very young.' And perhaps that sums it all up: I was very young.

'Yes, you were,' he says and there is a flicker of a smile, more in his eyes than his mouth.

I wonder what he is remembering: a body that was only about twenty, arching under and above his. Young skin, soft but taut like a sheet pulled tight. My face luminescent and watching him, taking him in. I did anything I could for him, to him, with him. He took it all and who could blame him?

I remember the gurgle of laughter in the back of his throat. It was laughter of surprise, delight. I remember the sudden snap of his intake of breath.

'It was perfect,' he says and his words appear as mist on the window.

My mother had been angry when she found out: giving him the best years of my life. That is how she described them, *the best years of your life*. And maybe they were and it's just as well that I didn't know it at the time. But standing here, with that gaze of remembering on his face and those lines in his face, I am pleased that I gave him something to remember.

'Well, almost,' he says, and turns and walks to the lounge. *It was perfect. Well, almost.*

I push my forehead against the glass of the window and it is impossibly cold, seeping into my brain.

'Can you shut the curtain? It's freezing out there,' he says.

I unhook the curtain from where it is pinned to one side. The curtain is white, transparent, and drops against the window with a quiet swoosh. I hear him put a log on the fire and, as he does, another log collapses. He swears softly. The poker clangs against the grate as he manoeuvres the wood.

A chill moves through me, all the way up my spine. I am still damp from the snow melting into my hair, my thin coat, and leaking into my boots and numbing my toes. I walk to the fire and sit on the rug beside his feet. He is standing with the poker hanging from his hand, staring at the fire mesmerised.

I pull off my boots and peel my wet woollen tights down my legs and drag them off. I push my legs straight in front of me; they are covered in goose bumps. My feet will soon be hot from the fire and I will be warm all the way through.

'How did you get so damp?' he asks.

'I got lost. I forgot the street.'

He hangs the poker back in its home against the tiles of the fireplace.

'I don't believe you,' he says.

He walks back to the lounge and leans against the arm, his feet crossed in front of him. It is a temporary position: he could be waiting for me to leave.

'What is there not to believe?' I say.

I am half turned so that I can see him, but his face is expressionless.

'I cannot believe that you forgot the street.'

He is right not to believe it.

I turn my back to him and pull a hand through my dark hair. It is the same colour as his, although he must have taken to colouring his. My hair is drying at the ends but is still wet at the crown. I hold my hair towards the fire and I can only see my knees and the edge of my red velvet skirt. I am like a child hiding my face, hiding so that I cannot be seen.

But I am here and so is he.

When I look up, he is draping my tights on a wooden chair beside the fire and has placed my boots so that their thin, sodden soles are facing the fire. He is helping me get ready to go.

A cat slinks into the room, orange fur and brilliant eyes. She stretches near my boots. He gently pushes his foot against the cat's stomach. She opens an eye and shuts it again. He calls her Betty, and I hear the smile in his voice. I don't want to ask him what happened to the one-eyed black cat, Mary. I presume she died. Witness, I called her for that was what she was, even if she only saw half of what was going on.

He is watching the cat.

'You came to this house every week for three years,' he says, still looking at the cat, not at me. 'I cannot believe you would forget this street,'

'You're right. I didn't forget.'

His gaze shifts from the cat to me.

'I walked around in the snow getting up the courage to come here. To see you.'

'Fuck. Suzanne.' His chest is rising and falling hard. 'Ten years.' He leaves the room.

It is perhaps the rudest thing a person can do to a married couple: sleep in the marital bed with one spouse whilst the other spouse is out earning money. The bed smelt of their sleep.

I told myself that life waited for no one, and it doesn't.

Thinking back, I don't know how I could do it to his wife and son, but they were unreal to me. She was perfume bottles on the dressing table and once a row of dark suits and silk shirts when the wardrobe door was left ajar. His son was small shoes in the entryway and a box of toys in the kitchen.

Neither of us had any money. I was a scholarship student living in a dormitory at a London university. He was writing a novel but I don't know whatever happened to it. As far as I know it was never published and I suspect that he gave up on it before anyone got a chance to reject it.

We met on Wednesdays: six hours when his wife was at work and his son was at preschool and, later, school.

Three years of Wednesdays. His body lying all along mine. Our hot mouths. Our limbs entangled. His tracing fingers. We were trapped together in that bed, until the allotted, cruel minute.

Even now, Wednesday has a different feel to it than any other day of the week. It is languorously stretched out in the middle of week: the middle of the working week and the middle of the seven day week. It is a day that seems to take so much longer than its twenty-four hours. Not then. Back then it was over in the blink of an eye.

A Wednesday morning, ten years ago, I arrived at his house. He opened the door and opened his mouth. I heard a voice call from inside, 'Who is it, Dad?'

I felt those words as a physical blow and stepped backwards.

His mouth closed and then opened to mouth, 'Sorry'.

But he reached forward and took my hand and lead me though the front door and into the lounge room. He dropped my hand just before the boy looked towards the doorway and saw me standing there beside his father.

'Henry. This is a friend of mine. Suzanne.'

Henry watched me, over the top of his book, as I followed his father into the room. He was reading an atlas. They were shortly taking a holiday to South Africa to see Isabel's family. I had those four weeks of family holiday marked in my calendar with large black crosses through each day, as if those days had already been lived, counted down, endured. As if they could be struck out by my pen.

Henry was wearing blue flannelette pyjamas with a cartoon fish emblazoned in a repeating pattern. He had kicked down to his feet a green woollen rug. The room smelt of Vicks. Mary lay at Henry's feet: the guardian of the child. Henry had the same dark hair as his father, but his liquid brown eyes were unrecognisable and I realised they must be from Isabel.

A finger darted up to push his black rimmed glasses higher onto his nose. It was the gesture of an old person.

'Hello Henry,' I said.

He kept up his watch and it was as if I had not said anything at all.

'Henry. Aren't you going to say hello?' his father said in a no-nonsense tone.

'Hello,' Henry said with a flat voice.

Mary watched me with her one eye; the other long removed. *Don't give me away, Mary*, I thought. She lay there, looking like she was thinking about it.

I realised that Henry could probably work things out for himself. A woman almost twenty years younger than his father, a *friend*, turning up at the house on a day when he should be at school and his mother was at work, toiling. A six-year-old boy can probably work these things out. Granted he could not see my ridiculously expensive black French lingerie or lace edged stockings that I wore under my nylon dress and coat. But he could probably guess at them. Little boys sometimes know more than they let on.

I turned to his father. 'I should go. I just popped by to give you this,' I said and dragged a novel from my bag and handed it to him. I cannot remember what it was now. It should have been *Anna Karenina*, *Madame Bovary*, or even *Lolita*, but I don't think it was anything so appropriate.

There was a look from him that I could not work out. He did not want me to leave, that much was clear. His hand fell on my arm. He seemed to see into me, maybe even into my poor bloody heart. He had not called me to warn me against coming over. Perhaps he thought we could get away with it. Or perhaps he wanted to take me upstairs and make me into a reality. And all the while those six-year-old eyes watched us from behind old man glasses.

I left the house and never returned. Not until now.

The lush pile of the rug against my bare legs reminds me that this house was built on considerable money earned by others. He has never properly belonged here, but still he stays.

Betty purrs contently before the hearth, half asleep.

I hear him cooking in the kitchen: a saucepan connecting with the stovetop, the chopping of vegetables on a wooden board. The aroma of onion and garlic sizzling in a pan triggers a pang of hunger.

He walks into the lounge room. His jacket is off, his sleeves rolled up.

'You'll stay to have dinner with me and Henry? He'll be back for dinner,' he says.

'Thanks. I would like that.'

He puts on the stereo: classical music. He opens a bottle of red wine and hands me a glass. I take the glass and I take his hand and pull him down toward me. Down. Down. Down. There is something of a giving in, the way his knees bend one at a time, lowering him to the floor, with his hand still in mine.

This is what I came here for. And how to tell him, *no one else has come close to you.*

He smiles and it is sweet and sad. He is on his knees as if he were praying about this one, which might not be a bad idea. He holds the side of my face with his cold hand. We kiss and when he opens his mouth, I dive in. His mouth tastes of red wine and him. I am taken over. Giddiness and excitement and nausea: that heady, familiar, cocktail floods my mouth and draws through my limbs and my blood. It is a homecoming. And maybe nothing has changed. Maybe nothing has changed after all.

Chris Fryer is making his first Fiction Desk appearance with this story. At least, I think it's his first...

The Loop

Chris Fryer

#234

Things are starting to get repetitive, for Sam more than the others.

'Have you ever looked into the eye of a devil?' he asks dramatically, one hand on the switch beside the black window. 'The eye of a devil?' he asks.

Rick grunts. Every time, a different grunt.

It always starts here in the observation room, overlooking the test chamber. Sometimes it starts after Sam gets shot, but usually we're just moments before the lights turn on. Usually we don't know about the gun yet.

Either way, it always takes me a moment to reassemble the mind, to recall where I am in the loop. In the end, I guess it doesn't matter, but a man goes a little crazy when he's not sure what universe he's in.

Our group is reflected in the glass at this slight angle that makes the four of us look like we have big heads, oversized brains, apt to burst. In subtle ways, I am starting to notice how we're falling apart. Our skin droops. Hair falls out. Clothing disintegrates. We are echoes far from their origin. Last time around the loop, I lost my wedding ring. Damn thing turned to dust.

Sam, smirking, always smirking, waits a moment and asks, 'Have you ever known true true true darkness?'

'Quit the bullshit,' says Rick, the engineer.

Gruff, honest, and far too old for space travel, Rick is my favourite member of the group. He called Sam's experiment a 'design flaw that could end all life as we know it,' and still he came along, probably just to say I told you so, which he would do plenty of times, not long from now.

'My apologies, Rick,' says smirking Sam. At this point, I can say what Sam will say before he says it. He shrugs twice. He says, 'I'm only only trying to prepare you. A lot of people, first time they see it, they burst into tears for no reason. First time I saw it, I couldn't sleep for a week. Couldn't sleep. Couldn't sleep.'

'Jesus, Sam. Thanks for the warning,' says my wife, Susan.

When our marriage counsellor told us to get more involved with each other's work, I don't think this was what was meant. Sam never said anything about bringing my wife along. In retrospect, this makes sense, but only Sam could make us believe it was important to have a historian on the moon.

Says Sam, 'Best to look in the corner of the room of the room first. Slowly bring your eyes to the centre, where you'll see see it floating there, staring back at you. First time I saw it, I couldn't sleep for a week.'

'Turn on the lights,' I say. 'We're ready.'

Rick says, 'Turn on the lights. We're ready.'

Sam looks at me, then Rick, brow furrowed with confusion, as if he isn't quite sure what he thinks he heard. The other thing I've learned is that the others are usually reset each time we switch universes, so unlike me, they don't know they've been trapped in an infinite loop.

I say, 'Impatience doesn't look good on you, Rick.'

Sam says, 'Impatience doesn't look good on you, Rick.'

Jacob, the activist, bites his lip and takes a small step backward. He's looking ill, but you can't tell if that's from motion sickness or the fact that he's died so many times recently. He should've never been invited here.

'Ladies and ladies and gentle gentlemen,' says Sam, the smirking scratched record, 'may I present to you, the first artificially created black hole.'

He flips the switch once, but I hear the click twice. Inside the test chamber, the lights flash, filling an enormous white cube, so pristine and flawless that the corners and edges are imperceptible, and there in the centre, an impossibly perfect black sphere, floating in a white prison.

Susan takes my hand and squeezes.

Sometimes she whispers, 'I can see myself.'

The eye of the devil never stops staring, and you can feel it like the strict gaze of a parent who has taught you to fear what has created you. It will consume and create us, recycle us, again and again and again until we are used up, dust.

Jacob pulls a gun and shoots Sam in the chest.

A few times, I tried to stop this from happening. A few times, I started the loop by shoving Jacob to the ground and taking his gun. But sometimes the gun wasn't there until he needed it: it would appear in his belt-loop like a bad film cut. Sam always wound up dead. Even if no gun went off, an exit wound would splash pieces of his spine across the observation window.

This time, I don't feel like interfering.

Susan screams. Rick stumbles backward, falling to his ass. He cries out, 'I fucking told you so!' Sam clutches at his chest as he slides down to the floor, smearing blood on the wall behind him, over the faint pink echo of earlier smears.

He says, 'Have you ever looked into the eye of the devil?'

'The devil?' he says.

Jacob shoots the window next. Impossibly fast, the window is vaporised, and just as quickly our bodies are yanked like kites into a tornado, stripped down to atoms inside the demon's pupil, crushed into a singular mass, erased entirely from existence. Then we are regurgitated, reformed, recycled.

Mike

I'm always first.

We become Mike Jenson. We are teaching fifth grade physics. We pass out tests that half the kids failed, saying things like, 'Good improvement, guys,' in my voice, our voice, this voice, one voice.

The bell rings. Thank God.

The students leave like there'd been a bomb threat. Oh so thankful for the respite of lunch break, we're quick to close the door behind George, also known as 'dandruff boy' whenever we talk to Susan about him.

Our stomach gurgles.

Susan made our lunch today. On the Susan diet, we eat no wheat. We open the paper bag to find an apple, a yogurt, and a Hershey kiss. This is the same thing we ate yesterday. We wonder, *Is this happiness for me?* We imagine divorcing her. We wonder where the passion went. Rumbling stomach aside, we throw the lunch away, and sometimes there are already crumpled brown lunch bags in there, echoes of earlier loops. Sometimes we eat the lunch and die a little.

We always end up at the vending machine in the teacher's office. We always flirt with the pretty substitute teacher with the southern accent and amber hair. We always pick something different from the machine. This time, Snickers.

On the walk back to our classroom, we watch a plane fly overhead and we wish that we could somehow transport into one of those seats and go wherever it was going, no matter where, no matter what.

Inside the room, there's Sam.

'Michael, Michael, Michael,' he says, opening his arms for a hug. Living in this neighbourhood, we're not used to suits and shiny shoes, so it takes a moment to place this billionaire in a shack of a classroom. 'You look surprised.'

'It's been a while.'

'Too long.'

'Are you just passing through?'

'Sit,' he says, pointing to my desk. 'You're the reason I'm here.'

We sit in the chair where our students normally sit while Sam takes the cushioned recliner we consider our throne, commandeering what is ours as he always has, the pompous prick. We feel like a dog trained by fear around him, like he might kick us if we didn't stay out of his way. We feel pathetic.

'I'm here to recruit you,' says Sam with a smirk full of small print.

'For what?'

'Your dream job. Your dream since college.'

'What's that?'

'Your dream since college,' he repeats.

We ignore the echo. 'I'm doing it already,' we lie.

He gives the classroom a quick once-over, then claps his hands. 'I need a logic man like you,' he says. 'A logic man like you. I've always been impressed with the way your mind works, Mike. You've got a mind like no one else.'

'I'm flattered.'

He reclines in our chair, puts his feet on our desk, and slowly folds his hands over his chest. 'You can see things at every angle. That's rare, I've come to find. I've come to find that's rare. People are so fixed these days. People lack creativity. They consider themselves logical but really that means really that means they've locked to one frame of mind. Allied with one answer. They've trapped themselves. Logic, Mike, logic is recognising there is more than one answer to every question.' He leans forward and says, 'I want you to help me find those answers.'

'I still have no idea what you're talking about,' we admit, noticing the clock on the wall, anticipating the end-of-lunch bell. We hate that bell. 'The kids will be back soon, Sam. I've got fifth period.'

'Beginner physics. I know.' Sam stands up. Sometimes his jacket is tattered and stained with blood. 'There's no interview process, Mike. If you say yes, you're on the team. We're leaving tomorrow morning. We're running the collider within the end of the month. I want you to be there for that.'

'Collider? You built a collider?'

'You thought I wouldn't?'

'For what?' we ask.

We can't believe our ears when Sam says, 'Making universes.'

Outside, the bell rings, but we barely hear it. We stand, always in the shadow of our old roommate, and looking up at him we say, 'Like we talked about.'

'Just like we talked about.'

We remember those long nights, stoned out of our minds, journals open and pencils scratching, writing down every exotic thought that crossed our minds. It was sophomore year we thought of the machine that could create new worlds, and we saw it then in Sam's glazed eyes that he would make it happen one day.

We shake hands.

Once Sam leaves, the kids arrive, and we stand at the front of the room and we wonder what Susan will think about this. With a smile, we realise that we don't really give a shit. We ask the students to pass in their homework.

Rick

We are cursing a wrench, condemning the tool to hell for all eternity, cursing this whole blasted engine, and for a second we're tempted to throw the piece-of-shit wrench across the hangar and give up for the day. But we are Rick and we never let a job go unfinished. We focus. We get the bolt tightened.

'Hey, Rick!' shouts a voice from the enormous open doors.

We moan. Third interruption this morning. Did they want this rocket fixed or not? A little privacy would've been nice. We hold up a hand to shield the glare of sun on cement, but can't tell who's coming.

'Yeah?'

The shape becomes a man, Sam, sometimes with bullet wound, always smirking, and he reaches out to shake our hand. We stare at those perfectly trimmed fingernails and we look at our own greasy hands, and we gladly spread some of the juice of manual labour into this bastard's soft palm.

'Got a towel?' asks Sam.

'On the cart behind you,' we say, nodding.

Sam wipes clean his hand and says, 'Let's start over.'

'A little late for that,' we say, and we remember the stolen patents, and we wonder how he hid his tracks, and we wish we wish we wish we could prove that he'd stabbed us in the back. We want to punch his face in.

'I have a job for you.'

We're stunned. 'You're really asking me this?'

He nods. 'We did it, Rick.'

'Did what?'

'We birthed a black hole.'

'It worked?'

'All systems stable.'

We want to smash that smirk off his skull with the wrench in our hand, but the bastard could be telling the truth. We ease off the anger. We ask questions. We want specifics. We're impressed. The bastard actually did it.

'Show me pictures.'

'That's the funny thing about it,' says Sam. 'That's the funny thing about it.'

We're not sure if we heard him twice, but it seems that way. We shrug the déjà vu aside and ask, 'About what?'

Sam says, 'I said the pictures never turn out. It's unphotographable.'

Sometimes Sam says, 'Have you ever known true darkness?'

We sense that something is wrong with him. There's an odd disconnect between his eye movement and his body movement, like a video where the audio is off sync and the lips are moving faster than the words form. We ask about other people he's told about this. We're the first. We want to know how soon we can leave.

He says, 'As soon as soon as you finish this rocket. Who do you think is funding the launch?'

We hate this man. We only recently finished paying off the debt owed for lawyers failing to get back what was ours, thanks to this one man, this man who we could kill with one swing. We offer a handshake to this devil.

'Rain check,' he says, smirking, walking away.

Sometimes we do kill him.

Susan

We are Susan. We are getting dressed. Suburban home. Los Angeles, California. We know these things, we have her thoughts. This morning we are so very happy our husband is not on this planet.

Black dress, pulled tight over our curves, we touch our breasts when we straighten the straps. We are happy with how we look. Kiss the mirror, leave red lipstick. We can't even remember the last time we wore this lipstick for Mike.

We take a taxi to a penthouse. Sam's penthouse.

He's not there, but we expected this. The doorman buzzes us in. We check our hair in the reflection of the elevator door, waiting, waiting, waiting, the numbers ticking down out of order, 29, 28, 27, 28, 27, 26, 25, until finally, ding, the doors open and we step inside, high heels clicking. We have a key to Sam's penthouse, we twist the knob with our manicured hands.

Spacious. Excessive. So very Sam.

We go immediately to the bedroom. We drape our coat over the back of a tall leather desk chair. The bed is full of pillows. Soft blankets. We've missed this bed, since Sam's been away. It hasn't been the same. We sigh. But this is still good.

Crawling into bed, we roll onto our back and find the remote control from the nightstand, and with this we turn on a large television. In a few minutes, Sam's face appears on the screen. Sometimes, he has blood dripping out of his mouth, but it's funny because we never mention the blood.

He's in his office, sitting now on a chair so that we see his whole body.

'My love dove,' he says.

'I've missed you,' we say in Susan's whine.

'We don't have much time.'

'I hate when you say that.'

Sam removes his shirt, one button at a time. We unzip our dress.

'Mike might suspect something.'

We roll our eyes. 'So what?'

We move our hands to our thin black underwear. Sam removes his pants. With the dip of a finger, we begin to writhe in pleasure on Sam's bed while he moans and strokes for us to watch 239,000 miles away.

Suddenly Sam says, 'Oh. Shit. Fuck. They're ready. They're calling me.'

We hear a buzz on his end of the line. He pulls on his pants and walks off screen to answer the phone. We stop fingering ourselves, leaving our hand there unfulfilled, letting out a long sigh. In our mind, we think, *This is the last time I do this.*

'Baby?' says Sam.

'Yeah?'

'I have to go, but but I have to ask you something.'

'Okay.'

'Will you come here? Will you join the team here?'

We thought he'd never ask. Without hesitation, nearly brought to tears, we tell him that of course we want to come. We couldn't stand going another eight months without fucking him for real.

'What will I do there?' we ask.

'You can be an outside consultant. With multiple universes, babe, you never know what part of history of history we might be able to visit.'

'And Mike?' we ask.

'I'll take care of Mike,' says smirking Sam. He buttons up his shirt. 'We're running the collider the collider again,' he says. 'I think we've got it figured out this time. I think this is the start of something big, love dove. I'll call you after to tell you all about it, and make plans for get getting you here.'

'I love you,' we say.

The screen goes white. We collapse into the soft blankets. We grin so wide it makes our eyes water. We laugh and roll about, feeling like a teenager intoxicated with first love. Sometimes, on the television, the eye of the devil appears, watching us from its prison in another universe, as if it has found us wandering.

Jacob

Our mouth is to a megaphone. We bark across the lawn, 'We're not put on this earth to destroy this earth!' We look at fellow protestors, cheering, clapping, our people, our brethren. We see Megan in the audience and our heart isn't the only muscle that grows at the sight of her.

We bark, 'Leave the destruction to the gods! We are not gods!'

Across the lawn looms the cement headquarters of Invotech, who every other week seem to push the boundaries of safe science, like kids playing with a toy chest full of nuclear warheads. We're ashamed to admit our father worked for them, a child like all the rest, luckily killed by cancer before doing anything irrevocable. We shake a fist in the air at that cement doomsday factory and bark, 'You can't decide the fate of the universe!'

No surprise, there's no media coverage. Some of the protestors are yawning. I want to tell them not to give up, but this is the eighth protest this year, and no one likes to come up empty handed that many times.

'Change takes time!' we yell, mostly to our fading peers.

Megan catches my attention, motioning for me to get off the stage.

We slip away from the crowd for a moment to kiss. She tastes like hot chocolate and lip balm. She shivers and we rub her arms and tell her she can go home if she wants, that we can handle this. She says, 'We're in this together.'

'I wonder if they'll send someone out,' we say.

'They never do.'

'Today feels different,' we say.

'People are starting to leave,' she says.

'It's not about quantity, Megan. Even if only one person shows up, that means someone cared enough to show up.' We see movement from the headquarters, a big door opening, and we think we see a car approaching. 'See that?' we ask.

'Someone's coming?'

The protestors behind us fall quiet, now hearing the engine of the car, a black sedan, slowly coming to a stop about ten yards from us. One male gets out. We recognise him immediately. Who wouldn't? It's Samuel Davidson, the founder, owner, devil himself.

'Mr Edwards?' calls out Sam.

'Yeah?'

'I'd like to speak with you privately, if you please.'

Megan squeezes our hand. Our heart pounds.

'Of course,' we call back, and we try to walk toward him but Megan is reluctant to release her grip. We kiss her, hold her face, her soft skin, grey eyes, and we tell her how much we love her.

She says, 'Don't trust him.'

We release her hand and approach the man by the sedan, who steps aside the back door with trained grace and says with a smirk, 'After you after you, Jacob.'

We get inside. Spacious. So very Sam.

The driver is hidden behind a black partition.

Sam slips into the seat across from us. We're offered a glass of merlot, the best glass of wine we've ever tasted. It warms the gut. Sometimes, we decline the wine, refusing the temptations of the devil. Sometimes it's chardonnay. Either way, he opens with the same line:

'Have you ever known true darkness?'

We think, *Do you count?*

We say, 'Have you ever known when enough is enough?'

'I've seen into the centre of the universe, Jacob.' Sam folds one leg over the other, straightening a wrinkle. 'I think there's plenty more to know.'

'At what cost?'

Sam shakes his head. 'You take this too personal.'

'You could destroy the universe.'

'Jacob, Jacob, Jacob...' he shakes his head. 'The universe will be fine.'

'If this is how you get us to stop protesting, it won't work.'

'I'm not here to stop you. I want to prove it to you.'

'Prove what?'

'That we're not monsters.'

We laugh. We think of dinner table conversations with our father about how science is God's way of telling us that we're capable of doing better, of outdoing God, of staking claim to the whole universe, manifest destiny style. We were sickened by the idea then, we're sickened by the idea now.

Sceptical, we ask, 'Prove it how?'

'I want you to come to the testing site. I want you to see into the eye.'

We cock our head to one side. 'The eye?'

Sam nods. He says, 'The eye of your creator, Jacob.'

Already we're thinking this is our chance. This is our chance. We've been out on this fucking lawn for months trying to get some attention, laughed at by the news media, ignored by all, and finally we get a break and it's better than we could've dreamed. There must be a catch, but we can't worry about that now. We lean forward and say, 'I don't know how you'll change my mind, but I'm willing to give you a chance, *Sam*.'

He smirks in reply, knocks on the partition window, and says, 'Garage.'

Sometimes, he says, 'First time I saw it, I didn't sleep for a week.'

Sam

Our hand hovers over the red button. We used to think it was cheesy design to make this button red, but, then again, if there was any button we didn't want to accidentally press, it was this one. A collider initiated without preparation could destroy the entire compound and leave a crater the size of Manhattan on the surface of the moon. We're glad the button stands out.

'Ready when you are,' says Hank.

'Cameras rolling?' we ask.

'Affirmative.'

'Shields up?'

'Of course, sir.'

We feel the energy of the button beneath our palm. We envision the wealth and fame of a successful test. We rationalise a failure. *This is only the first test, this is only the first test*, we repeat in our buzzing mind.

'Sir?' says Hank.

'I'm fine. On three.'

We count down to one. Sometimes we have last-second concerns that we're about to destroy the entire known universe. Sometimes we imagine receiving a Nobel Prize before a crowd of thousands, thanking our family, our friends, our colleagues. Either way, we press the red button.

In the chamber below, invisible to the eye, atoms explode. Atoms reassemble. Atoms are crushed, exploded, eviscerated, expanded, stretched, and broken. Dimensions are twisted. In less than less than an instant, a black sphere appears in the middle of the chamber, floating, suspended by electromagnets, the size of a basketball. In a blink it is gone.

We aren't even aware that we've fallen over. Hank, too. We pick ourselves up from the carpet and move to the window. The test chamber is empty.

'Wild,' Hank says. He wipes sweat off his brow. Then he wipes sweat off his brow again.

'It worked for a second,' we say.

'Did you see it?' asks Hank.

We think a moment, then reply, 'It was more like it saw me.'

'I know how you feel.'

'What do you think went wrong?' we ask, picturing a thousand different things that could be altered, from the strength of the magnets, the position of the sun relative to the moon, to the unpredictability of subatomic chaos.

Hank says, 'Maybe it just needs to be faster.'

We laugh. 'Crank it up, then.'

He leaves the room to consult the staff. We lean against the wall, staring at the red button, thinking of people we could bring up here to help.

We think about Mike Jenson, though we try not to, seeing as we're fucking his wife. He was a brilliant kid in college, just never took advantage of it. We picture him begging for a chance to work with us.

What about Rick Carson? He'd know how to fix the collider better than anyone. Even if he's still sore about that business with the patent lawsuit, he'd never let this opportunity pass him by. We think about trying to get some snapshots from the video feed, for proof, since Rick might want to bash our head in with a wrench before taking our word for it.

We look down into the test chamber.

Sometimes it's empty. Sometimes, the eye is looking back at us.

#235

In the next instant, Sam is dying on the floor, gripping his gunshot wound, and he doesn't look very surprised. We're separate again, touching our bodies, mystified by the concept of individual existence, individual minds.

During some loops, I'm not the only one who remembers.

I recall immediately that Sam was fucking my wife, and my wife, Susan, she turns to me because she knows what I've seen, and Rick, he wishes he still had that wrench. Jacob is in the middle of the room staring at the gun in his hand.

Wind is whistling through a bullet hole in the glass. In this universe, the glass is stronger. Here, we always get a little more time. Sometimes Jacob shoots himself in the throat. Sometimes he kills all of us. This time, he says, 'The fate of the universe is not in our hands.'

Sam groans, 'I couldn't sleep for a week.'

I look at Susan and say, 'I wish you would've told me.'

For a moment, she's more beautiful than anything I've ever seen. She lets a tear roll down her face and she says, 'I didn't want to hurt you.'

Jacob says, 'We are not meant for weapons of mass destruction.'

He shoots Sam in the face.

Rick is crawling across the floor. When he passes, he says, 'I fucking told him this would happen.' He adds, 'There's an emergency shutdown button on the desk. I think we have time.'

I say, 'Don't bother.'

Jacob says, 'Our first sin was creating fire.'

Then he shoots himself. Behind him, splattered in red, the window cracks a little more, the devil's eye pulling at our souls. Rick arrives at the desk. He presses the emergency shutdown button.

I turn to Susan and say, 'I want a divorce.'

Then the black hole explodes. Everything is made to nothing.

#236

Things are starting to get repetitive, more for Sam than anyone.

'Have you ever looked into the eye into the eye of a devil?' he asks, smirking.

Nik Perring has written several volumes of very short fiction, and is gaining recognition as one of the masters of this deceptively difficult genre. This is his first Fiction Desk appearance.

Loss Angina
Nik Perring

A couple of months after Jude left, the man shaved off his lips. Won't be needing these anymore, he said to himself, standing before the bathroom mirror, razor in hand, the tap dripping.

It was quick and it didn't hurt too much; it wasn't half as painful as knowing he would never kiss her again. But that dull, hollow ache in his heart he'd almost become used to, like it was an illness or disease. He put up with it. Accepted it. It was like loss angina or love arthritis or something. It was painful and it was there to stay.

He had expected people to notice his changed face, but no one said a word when he went to buy his morning paper, and there were no funny looks in the coffee shop where he stopped to read it. The waitress smiled at him as she usually did, her lips full and red, as she refilled his cup before tottering back behind the counter.

Back home and he was in front of his mirror again.

It is *noticeable*, he decided. Not horrific, not like something from a horror movie or like someone just returned from a war zone. The skin around his mouth was smooth. It just looked empty. It was simply: noticeable. And, as such, the man wanted people to notice.

So, when he next went to the shop to buy his morning paper he made sure he struck up a conversation as he paid. He even whistled at the headline, to draw attention to what was not there. But still, nothing.

Things were no different at the coffee shop either. He even smacked what used to be his lips when he told the waitress how tasty her croissants smelled. But again, infuriatingly: nothing.

So he sat down and he flicked his paper's pages and he did not read their words because his mind was busy thinking, and when the waitress came over and offered him a refill he said, 'Yes please. But, before you do, could I ask you something?'

'Sure,' she told him, so he said, 'Do you notice anything different about my face?'

The waitress shrugged. Shook her head. Her hair swayed.

'Can't you see?' he said, placing the paper on the table top, leaning towards her, enunciating every word. 'I have no lips!'

'A lot of the people who come in here are missing something,' she said. 'Lots have lost things. That's why I only look at their eyes. They say much more than anything else can.'

'But I didn't *lose* my lips,' the man protested, louder now so that people were turning in their seats to look and to listen. 'I shaved them off!'

'Shush, honey,' she replied. Her words were warm. 'You've lost something all right. Believe me. Like I said, it's all in the eyes.' She smiled then, said, 'Now, how about that top-up?'

And the man returned her smile, as best he could, and he nodded and he returned to his paper. Flicked its pages from cover to cover but, as he did, he did not read one single word. His mind was elsewhere. It was busy, missing.

'Bing Bong' is Jo Gatford's first story for The Fiction Desk, and took first place in our 2014 flash fiction competition. Appropriate, then, that she should play us out with a little music.

Bing Bong
Jo Gatford

When he was five you took him to see the steam train. To hear the whistle: a perfect D sharp, held longer than he expected, snapped off in mid-air but left ringing inside the steam. Water music. Then it was 'McDonalds, Mama,' because he said the sound of the fryers mixed with the pop songs piped overhead and formed a mountain range that he rode up and down with his arm outstretched, like riding airwaves out the window of a moving car.

You took him to the barber's twice a month and they were too embarrassed to charge you for 'just a tiny trim' because it was only really the buzz of the clippers he wanted curving around the back of his ear.

'You could do this at home for free,' the hairdresser said. You shook your head. He needed the squeak of the chair and the phut-phut of the hydraulics when they pumped him up to the top height, little shoes dangling from skinny puppet legs in perfect rhythm with the snip of the scissors.

You took him to the doctor. 'The same CD as last time,' he said, as you sat in the waiting room. *Total Eclipse of the Heart, Sweet Caroline, Hi Ho Silver Lining*. And, 'That man's cough sounds like he's harmonising with himself.' And, 'The bing-bong when they call your name, make them do it again, Mama.'

'I can't,' you told him, deflecting well-meaning smiles from other patients.

'I need to hear it again,' he said, louder.

'Shush now.'

'But I need to, Mama,' he said, as if he were in pain. So you asked at reception if they could press the button for him, but they gave you the same look his teacher gave you when she told you about the incident in assembly. 'Obnoxious,' the accompanist had called him, curling her tongue, 'Criticised by a five-year-old!' *Sing Hosanna to the King of Kings* was his favourite, he told you, but the grumpy old cow at the piano had 'lazy fingers, Mama. She didn't move fast enough. I just wanted to show her how to do it better.' So you took him to the doctor because his teacher suggested that you should in a don't-worry-but-this-could-be-serious kind of way.

'They'll press the bell when it's time to call you in,' the receptionist said, and turned her eyes down to paperwork she'd already finished.

'You have a button right there,' you told her, fingernail pushed up against the safety glass that separated you. 'Right there. That's the one, isn't it?'

He sat where you'd left him, a good boy really, listening to the patter of his tears as they landed on his shorts, sniffing long and hard to hear the birds that sometimes tweeted inside his nostrils. 'My nose is a wind instrument,' was his first joke. Your father-in-law was round for dinner: mashed potatoes and chicken pie. 'Chickens don't fly but they make a fluttery flappery flit flit sound when they try.'

Your father-in-law spoke like the boy wasn't there. 'There's something wrong with this... aural obsession.'

'But it is an instrument, Grandpa, even yours. You can blow it, you can trumpet it, you can even make a sound when you breathe in. Mine will be even louder when it's as big as yours.'

You didn't laugh at the time but you wanted to now.

'Please,' you said, reaching your hands under the glass, across the counter. You'd cut into the queue and you didn't care.

The receptionist said she was sorry but she wasn't at all. 'If you take a seat —'

And you knew how it would go if you went into that doctor's office. Take a seat. Take a pamphlet. Take a consultation with a specialist. Take a pill, take a label, take your son out of his world and make him fit into a quieter one. 'Press the fucking button,' you whispered.

'I beg your pardon?'

'Press the button just once, for a little boy who likes the bing-fucking-bong, and then we will leave without me screaming so loud I break this glass.'

The receptionist looked at you and then at your son and you realised she had no idea about music beyond the Swingin' Sixties compilation that she was forced to listen to thirty times a day, and you pitied her.

Perhaps she felt it. She pressed the button.

And 'bing-bong,' your boy sang, in a tone like rainwater.

About the Contributors

Die Booth lives in Chester, in a tiny house with four fireplaces and enjoys toy cameras and exploring dark places. Die's work has featured in various anthologies including three Cheshire Prize for Literature collections and the co-edited 2011 project *Re-Vamp*. Die's first novel *Spirit Houses* – an action-packed tale of possession, betrayal and excellent Scotch – is out now.

Future projects include stories featured in *Chaperon Rouge: the Art of Fairytales* edited by Sarah Grant, and a single author flash fiction collection scheduled for release in late 2014.

Alex Clark holds an MA in archaeology and spent her early working years as an historic buildings archaeologist. She has been employed on sites ranging from Sheffield cutlery factories to the Olympic Park, and would like it to be know that the working conditions depicted in 'The Stamp Works' are pretty accurate. In 2009 she retrained as a restoration stonemason and moved to

Cheltenham, where she currently lives with her husband. 'The Stamp Works' is Alex's first published story.

Peter Clarke lives and works in Oxfordshire. He has an MA in Creative Writing from the University of Southampton. His stories have previously been published in *The Cadaverine* and *Pastiche Magazine*.

James Collett is 29, very skint, quite bitter, and good at rolling cigarettes. He lives, mostly on beans, in Cheltenham, and has never had any failed marriages, nor any successful ones. He retired from shelf-stacking and alcoholism two years ago and now writes full-time for almost no money. He never does anything useful.

Sarah Evans has had dozens of stories published in magazines, competition anthologies and online. Highlights of her writing career include: appearing in the 2008 Bridport anthology; having several stories published in the highly acclaimed Unthology series, published by Unthank books; winning a short story competition run by Spoken Ink who also recorded her story. She has also had stories published by Bloomsbury, Writers' Forum, Earlyworks Press, Rubery Press and many more.

Sarah lives in Welwyn Garden City with her husband and her interests include walking and opera.

Chris Fryer is a traveler and a teacher, using the lessons he learns along the way and the people he meets abroad to inspire his stories. A California native, he currently lives in Japan. He had been published by *Best New Writing*, the *Calaveras Journal*, *Lamp Light*, and the *Copperfield Review*.

Jo Gatford wants to live on your bookshelf. Her debut novel, *White Lies*, will be published by Legend Press in July 2014. You can find her short stories and flash fiction in *Litro*, *Open Pen*, *SmokeLong Quarterly*, and elsewhere. She lives in Brighton where she wrangles two insomniac children and writes sweary social media content for rude cartoonists.

Cindy George was first published as a writer of short stories for *Just Seventeen* magazine in the late eighties, and as a music journalist for the *NME* and others in the fallow period between acid house and Britpop. She worked in radio advertising for many years, and has also been a press officer and a farmhand on a banana plantation. She has an MA in Writing from Warwick University, and is working on her first novel.

Melissa Goode lives in the Blue Mountains just outside of Sydney, Australia. She has been published in *Best Australian Short Stories* and a short film was recently made based upon one of her stories. She is currently working on a novel.

Edmund Krikorian is a trainee solicitor who has only very recently started writing fiction, and who dreams of one day escaping the rat race. He writes about anything that interests him, but tends towards science fiction and the unlimited possibilities it contains. He has been published in *Crannog Magazine*, and has a paid blog at lawcareers.net. He has written several short stories, and is currently working on a first novel.

Nik Perring is a short story writer and author. His stories have been published in many fine places both in the UK and abroad, in print and online. They've been used on High School distance learning courses in the US, printed on fliers, and recorded for radio. Nik is the author of the children's book, *I Met a Roman Last Night, What Did You Do?* (EPS, 2006); the short story collection, *Not So Perfect* (Roastbooks 2010); and he's the co-author of *Freaks!* (The Friday Project/HarperCollins, 2012). *Beautiful Words*, his latest, is out now. His online home is www.nikperring.com and he's on Twitter as @nikperring.

Dan Purdue's short stories have been published in print and online in the UK, Ireland, Canada, and the United States, in places such as *The View From Here*, *Jersey Devil Press*, *The New Writer*, *Every Day Fiction*, *Southword*, and *The Guardian*. His work has won prizes in a variety of competitions, featured in an English study guide, and been broadcast on hospital radio. Dan lives in Leamington Spa in the West Midlands, and you can find him online at lies-ink.blogspot.co.uk or on Twitter at @DanPurdue.

Mark Taylor writes short stories, novels, cryptic crosswords, and bad puns. He studied English at the University of Cambridge and is part of the South East London Writers' Group.

Mike Scott Thomson's short stories have been published by a number of journals and anthologies, including those from *Litro*, *Prole*, *The Momaya Annual Review*, and *Stories for Homes* (in aid of the housing charity Shelter). 'Me, Robot,' his story to feature in The Fiction Desk anthology *Crying Just Like Anybody*, was also adapted for performance by the theatre group Berko Speakeasy. Competition successes include the runner up prizes in both the Inktears Short Story Competition (2012) and the Writers' Village International Short Fiction Competition (2013).

Based in Mitcham, Surrey, he works in broadcasting.

For more information on the contributors
to this volume, please visit our website:

www.thefictiondesk.com/authors

Various Authors
the first Fiction Desk anthology

Charles Lambert	Matthew Licht
Lynsey May	Ben Lyle
Jon Wallace	Danny Rhodes
Patrick Whittaker	Harvey Marcus
Adrian Stumpp	Alex Cameron
Jason Atkinson	Ben Cheetham

ISBN 9780956784308

All These Little Worlds
the second Fiction Desk anthology

Charles Lambert	Colin Corrigan
Jason Atkinson	Ryan Shoemaker
Halimah Marcus	Jennifer Moore
Andrew Jury	Mischa Hiller
James Benmore	

ISBN 9780956784322

The Maginot Line
the third Fiction Desk anthology

Benjamin Johncock	Matt Plass
Ian Sales	Shari Aarlton
Claire Blechman	Mandy Taggart
Andrew Jury	Justin D. Anderson
Harvey Marcus	

ISBN 9780956784346

Crying Just Like Anybody
the fourth Fiction Desk anthology

Colin Corrigan	Mike Scott Thomson
S R Mastrantone	Miha Mazzini
Die Booth	William Thirsk-Gaskill
Matthew Licht	Luiza Sauma
Matt Plass	Richard Smyth

ISBN 9780956784360

Because of What Happened
the fifth Fiction Desk anthology

Matt Plass	Gavin Cameron
Cindy George	Damon King
Tim Lay	James Collett
Ian Shine	Robert Summersgill
Paul Lenehan	Andrew Jury
Tania Hershman	Warwick Sprawson
S R Mastrantone	Tony Lovell
Ian Sales	

ISBN 9780956784384

New Ghost Stories
the sixth Fiction Desk anthology

Julia Patt	Richard Smyth
Eloise Shepherd	Ann Wahlman
Oli Hadfield	Linda Brucesmith
Matthew Licht	Jonathan Pinnock
Jason Atkinson	Miha Mazzini
Amanda Mason	Joanne Rush

ISBN 9780992754709

Subscribe

three volumes for just **£22**

(in the UK, or £29 worldwide).

Subscribing to our anthology series is the best way to keep yourself supplied with the best new short fiction from the UK and abroad. It costs just £22 for three volumes within the UK, or £29 for a worldwide subscription.

We publish a new volume roughly every four months. Each one has its own title: *There Was Once a Place* is volume seven.

Subscribe online:

www.thefictiondesk.com/subscribe

(Price correct at time of going to press, but may change over time; please see website for current pricing.)